Year of the Dog

Henry Chang

Published by
Soho Press, Inc.
853 Broadway
New York, NY 10003

Library of Congress Cataloging-in-Publication Data
Chang, Henry, 1951–
Year of the dog / by Henry Chang.
p. cm.
ISBN 978-1-56947-515-7
1. New York (N.Y.). Police Dept.—Fiction. 2. Chinese—United States—
Fiction. 3. Chinatown (New York, N.Y.)—Fiction. I. Title.
PS3603.H35728Y43 2008
813'.6—dc22
2008018856

10   9   8   7   6   5   4   3   2   1

Year of the Dog

Also by the author

Chinatown Beat

For Mom, who crossed the oceans with quiet courage, leaving behind a war-torn nation, bound for America, to a Chinatown life of piecework, sweatshops, and family. May the *Kwoon Yum*, Goddess of Mercy, stand beside you always.

Acknowledgments

A blood-thick thanks to Andrew, my brother, the first-born son, for his patience, understanding, and PC Photoshop skills.

A heartfelt thanks to Laura Hruska, my Soho editor, for her keen insight which undoubtedly has elevated my words.

Deep appreciation to Dana and Debbie who continue to believe in the stories.

Great gratitude to Sophia, Mimi, and Bobo, for maintaining the machine.

And as always, love to all my Chinatown brothers, past and present. They inspire me every day.

The Year of the Dog

The Dog is the eleventh sign, next to last in the lunar cycle, the most likeable of all the animals. The Dog is fearless, charismatic, and believes in justice, loyalty, and fidelity.

The year is characterized in the masculine Yang, by struggle, perseverance, and faith.

O-Nine

The Ninth Precinct started at the East River, and ran west to Broadway. On the north it was bounded by Fourteenth Street; on the south, Houston. Within these confines, the neighborhoods were the East Village, Loisaida, NoHo, Alphabet City, and Tompkins Square. Anarchists, artists, students, and the low-income working class all lived together, sometimes tenuously, until their breaking points made the *Daily News* headlines.

The detectives who worked in the Ninth were accustomed to dealing with multicultural scenarios, the daily struggles of blacks and whites, browns and yellows. The scattered Asian presence within its boundaries consisted mostly of hole-in-the wall Chinese take-out joints, Korean delis and dry cleaners, Japanese sushi spots, and even what was probably the last Chinese hand laundry in New York. In the Village, Southeast Asians peddled T-shirts, punk-rock jewelry, and drug paraphernalia. Indians and Pakistanis ruled over the newspaper stands.

Jack Yu had been assigned to the Ninth to cover the holidays. He leaned back from his computer desk in the detective's area and closed his eyes. On Thanksgiving Day, the last hour of the overnight shift was the longest. His nagging fatigue was spiked with uneasy anticipation.

Homicides in Manhattan South, or diverted from Major Case, were only a phone call away.

He pressed his trigger finger against his temple, working tight little circles there. Computer statistics scrolled dimly inside his forehead, the blunt, logical CompStat analysis of why and how people killed each other in New York City.

There were hundreds of murders in the five boroughs each year; closer to two thousand in the early days of crack cocaine. The records indicated that people killed because of:

Disputes 28%
Drugs 25%
Domestic violence 13%
Robbery/Burglary 12%
Revenge 10%
Gang related 8%
Unknown 4%

Entire lifetimes were reduced to an NYPD short list of cold percentages, time and location, gender and ethnicity.

Just the facts. Leave the speculation to the beat dicks.

The statistics indicated that *women were more likely than men to murder a spouse or lover,* and:

Male killers favored firearms over all other weapons.
Brooklyn, a.k.a. Crooklyn, had more killings citywide than any of the other five boroughs. 46%.
Saturday was the most popular day both for killing and dying.
Men and boys perpetrated 90% of the murders.
The deadliest hour was between one and two AM.
In half the cases, the killer and victim knew each other.

In 75% of cases, the perp and the vic were of the same race.
Homicides were concentrated in poorer neighborhoods.
Most of the killers had criminal records.
A third of homicides went unsolved.

Asians, who made up 11 percent of the city's population, accounted for 4 percent of the victims, and oddly enough, for 4 percent of the killers. The number four, in spoken Chinese, sounded like the word for *to die*.

Jack knew working the Ninth Precinct, the *0-Nine*, wouldn't be like working anticrime in Brownsville, or East New York, where killings were commonplace, and cops were used to tabulating bodies on a weekly basis. The 0-Nine, according to the Compstat analysis, didn't have a lot of homicides, but kept pace with other precincts with regards to all other types of incidences, like armed robberies, burglaries, domestic disputes, teen violence, and drug dealing.

He grabbed at and massaged the knotted cords in the back of his neck, taking a deep boxer's breath through his nose.

The 0-Nine house seemed to be a good fit for him, a welcome surprise. He wasn't expecting any of the problems he'd had in the Fifth Precinct. He figured that his exploits there, which had earned him a gold shield, would have preceded him to the new stationhouse, earning him a small measure of respect.

Jack got up from the desk and went toward the rear window, smoothly swinging his hips and legs down into a *long bridge* squat, a Shaolin-style stretch. His lower joints and ligaments popped as he straightened up, watching the frozen gray Alphabet City morning seep in through the window.

One call came into the precinct. A junkie from the projects had been found dead of an apparent drug overdose in an Avenue D shooting gallery, but Narcotics swept it up as part of a larger operation. The dead junkie was their CI, their confidential informant.

The remainder of the shift passed quietly, punctuated only by crackling voices from the squad radio at the duty desk out front. Nobody killed anyone in the precinct on this overnight shift, but on the Lower East Side, Jack knew, violence was only one wrong look, one bad intention away.

Out by the duty desk, the uniforms of the day shift rolled in.

Jack signed out as they started to muster for roll call. He was thinking of the hot chowder at Kim's when the first frigid gust of East River wind slapped him in the face.

Bodega Koreano

Kim's Produce was a mom-and-pop Korean deli on Tenth Street, a few blocks from the Ninth Precinct stationhouse. It was 9:18 AM on the Colt 45 display clock, well past his twelve-hour tour, when Jack joined the cashier's line with his take-out container of hot clam chowder. A small television set showed the Thanksgiving Day parade. He sipped the steaming soup as he waited, watching the TV. Jack had mixed thoughts about the holiday seasons in the city. These were celebrations, but for many people the seasons were very sad times. There were two cities here—one rich, one poor, each spiritually if not physically segregated from the other.

Jack watched the Macy's Parade march down Central Park West, past the stately and formidable buildings whose names rolled out: Majestic, Prasada, Dakota, San Remo, the landmarks of the rich and fabulous, private balconies with front-row views. The majorettes fronting the marching bands moved briskly down through the Twentieth Precinct, toward the old Mayflower Hotel, then on past Trump International, where top-shelf guests reserved midlevel suites for *holiday packages* at a thousand a night, so that their children would be thrilled by the giant cartoon balloons floating past their floor-to-ceiling double-paned glass windows. The Pink Panther. The Cat in the Hat. Barney the Dinosaur. Sonic the Hedgehog, who had an appetite for lamp-posts along Central Park.

Down below, at street level, two million of the hoi polloi gathered along the parade route, crowded and penned-in along the sidewalks, in the bitter cold. Tourists and middle-class families from the outer boroughs saw the floats rolling by—Big Bird and Santa Claus, and comic-book heroes floating in the sky.

The parade moved south toward Times Square, passing through the Midtown Commands, Manhattan North and Manhattan South. It would all end, Jack knew, at the Macy's store at Herald Square, where there would be backup from the Tenth and Thirteenth Precincts, and, of course, plenty of overtime uniforms managing the crowds, working the barricades and the subways.

Much farther downtown, Jack knew, there were no luxurious hotel rooms, no balloons or floats. On the Lower East Side,

Loisaida, the holidays found citizens of the 0-Nine at soup kitchens and food pantries, at the Bowery Mission, where the hungry, homeless families and the poor eagerly awaited a traditional hot turkey meal with all the trimmings, with the rest of the citizenry giving thanks, *There but for the grace of God go I*. Holy Cross, St. Mary's, St. Mark's Shelter: Soup kitchens scattered throughout the precinct gave them all something to be thankful for, even for one day.

The holidays were a humbling time for them; the displays of cheery celebration, and religious and commercial spectacles were not theirs. To them it was only another year of struggle passing by.

In Chinatown, most Chinese people didn't celebrate a traditional Thanksgiving, but the holiday provided an excuse for them to get together and feast on a meal of seafood, pork, chicken, and baby bok choy. Lobster Cantonese instead of turkey, rice instead of mashed potatoes, with winter melon and lotus root soup. Extended families gathered around *da bean lo*, hot-pot casserole-style cooking.

Jack didn't have fond memories of the holidays. Pa had never felt he had a lot to give thanks for, and hadn't been a big believer in Christmas either, so Jack rarely received gifts. His one big thrill had been getting something from the Fifth Precinct PAL, when he'd line up with all the other "deprived" Chinatown kids hoping for a holiday handout. He remembered one year getting trampled in the mad rush of the older kids and parents to get a free toy. *Trampled for a Popeye-the-Sailorman figure*. He cried, but was still happy to have the free gift. When he brought it home, Pa had derided him for getting run over for a stupid *gwailo* doll.

Jack reached the cashier at the same time that his cell phone jangled and broke his reverie. He paid for his soup, and flipped open the phone.

It was the dayshift duty sarge, telling him patrol had responded to a call and found multiple bodies, very dead, at One Astor Plaza, down from the Barnes & Noble bookstore.

Sergeant Donahoe was in the blue-and-white downstairs at the scene.

Manhattan South was responding to holiday road rage auto fatalities on the Westside Highway, so they were reaching out to Jack.

"On my way," Jack said, pocketing the phone.

He finished the soup in a big swallow, turned up his collar, and emerged onto the frozen street. He made his way west, through the East Village, the icy wind already tearing at his face, icy needles prickling his eyes every step of the way.

Face and Death

One Astor Plaza was a twenty-story curved glass tower, a luxury high-rise condominium building seamlessly shoehorned into the middle of a neighborhood crossroads that spread out to include the Public Theater, the NYU and Cooper Union campuses, the East Village and NoHo. It was a doorman residence, had security in the lobby, and a concierge behind a black marble counter. A Commercial Bank branch anchored the rest of the main street floor. A two-bedroom unit cost 1.5 million dollars and the project had sold out during construction.

The sculpted neo-modern glass building towered over the main avenues that ran north-south through Manhattan, over the major eastside subway hub, and dominated that entire commercial corner of Cooper Square.

A big overweight man, Sergeant Donahoe, stepped out of the squad car.

"I've got Wong up there," he said.

Police Officer Wong, Jack knew, was a rookie patrolman, a Chinese-American portable who could speak several Chinese dialects.

"Eighteen-A," Donahoe continued. "You got the building manager, the security guard, the grandmother, all up there. The fire lieutenant's at the fireboard in the lobby. Talk to him first."

Jack sucked in a deep gulp of cold air. "What do you have?" he asked, steeling himself.

Donahoe gave him a sad look and shook his gray-haired head.

"It's the whole family . . ." He paused and before he could continue, Jack had turned and was heading for the lobby.

The fire lieutenant, another tall Irishman, explained that they'd come to the scene because a ceiling smoke detector had activated and the alarm had gone out through the fireboard.

"When we got to the floor, there was no smoke," he said. "But the ceiling detector was a combination type that also detected carbon monoxide."

"So it was the carbon monoxide that set it off?" Jack asked.

"We took several readings," the lieutenant said. "The CO levels were over eighty parts. And ten parts is unsafe."

"Eight times lethal," Jack noted.

"Hell of a thing on Thanksgiving Day. Anyway, my men are

done upstairs." The lieutenant added, "We're just resetting the fireboard now."

"Thanks for your help," Jack said, grateful for the heads up as to what he was walking into.

Jack had heard many other cops deride the firefighters as thieves, referring to how they would take money and property from fire scenes. Quite often control of a crime scene that involved a fire was contested between the two commands, cops versus firefighters. Jack never saw it; he thought the firefighters had a tough job entering burning buildings, especially in winter. Even though he knew that the FDNY was still segregated—mostly white, mostly Irish—he had to give them respect for the hazardous jobs they did.

The elevators were fast, industrial quality steel polished into an elegant design.

The door to 18A was open, with yellow Crime Scene tape running across it. The firefighters had cranked open all the windows and evacuated all the residents of the eighteenth floor. P.O. Wong stood by the door with the building manager who nervously jangled a set of master keys. Jack introduced himself to the manager, nodded to Wong.

"I'll need a statement from you," he said to the manager. "Also, the security report, and information about the tenants."

The manager was in shock. His face was pallid, voice shaky. He said sadly, "Certainly. I'll be in my office on the main floor. It's a terrible, terrible thing." He walked slowly to the elevator.

Wong, who was shorter than Jack and built like a bulldog, pulled off one end of the yellow tape.

Jack asked him, "Wong, when accidents happen, do you think it's destiny?"

P.O. Wong answered, "Well, this sure wasn't an accident, but it could be destiny." A puzzled look cross Jack's face when he saw the Chinese grandmother seated on a folding chair just outside the apartment door.

"We had a hard time calming her down," Wong told him. "She only speaks Taiwanese."

Jack put his pen to his notepad. "Tell it," he said quietly, glancing at the old woman.

"Grandma there gets a panicked phone call from Taiwan," Wong began. "The in-laws are freaking out that something bad was going to happen here. They had received a letter from their son, the tenant, just today."

Jack looked up from his pad.

"It sounded like he was saying good-bye," Wong continued.

The old woman glanced at Jack, who was running worst-case scenarios in his mind.

"It took her a coupla hours to get here from Jersey," Wong went on. "And then there was a delay at the front desk, the language problem, and they wanted to make sure who she was, things like that. They called upstairs, there was no answer. Then the building manager came up with the grandma and security, and used his master keys. Both locks were locked. When they opened the door the corridor detector went off."

"So then the fire department arrived," Jack commented.

"A few minutes after. So then we went into the apartment."

Jack stepped inside the apartment, followed by Wong. At their feet was a crumpled-up quilt, crushed against the inside of the door.

The old woman still sat in stunned silence as they passed her. Jack scanned the room. It was very cold inside. The windows were wide open and lightweight curtains danced in the wind. Jack noticed an aquarium with eight Chinese goldfish floating belly up.

The floors were covered with off-white carpeting throughout.

The big room beyond, the open living room, was bathed in the dull gray morning light that flooded in through floor-to-ceiling windows, a flat wash that muted the few touches of color the room held. The modern, understated furniture consisted of a navy-blue L-shaped couch with a matching ottoman at one end, a wide-screen television, and a glass coffee table. One wall held a built-in shelf unit that displayed porcelain vases, terra-cotta figurines of Chinese men on horseback, and a miniature red, white, and blue flag of Taiwan. Everything was neat, like a deluxe hotel room after a maid had been through it. To one side was a kitchen area, set off by an island with a granite countertop that housed a sink and dishwasher. A stainless-steel refrigerator and matching cabinets lined the walls.

At the far end of a hall were the bedrooms.

Wong continued, "The son's letter described some bad business deals, and told them he'd lost money in the stock market."

Spread across the range top and the granite counters were an array of saucepans, and two small Chinese woks. There were ashes and charred lumps in all of them. Jack saw a box of wooden kitchen matches and a small can of lighter fluid. Someone had cooked up eight containers of charcoal briquettes on the range, dousing them up with lighter fluid to keep them all going.

"There's an empty bag of charcoal behind the counter," Wong said. "The son and his wife were depressed over their losses." He continued, "The two children went to a fancy private school."

Jack walked into the smaller bedroom.

"How old were the kids?" he asked.

"Five and six," Wong said solemnly. "Two little boys." He was disciplined enough to brief Jack with the factual information, but smart enough to keep his opinions and personal feelings to himself.

The boys' room had twin beds with New York Yankees pillow shams and matching duvet covers. Between the two beds was a nightstand with a Mickey Mouse table lamp. A desk held a computer and over it were shelves full of children's books. Stuffed animals were displayed on the dresser and a few large ones stood on the carpet: Pooh Bear and Tigger, Barney and Big Bird. Posters of Thomas the Tank's adventures hung on the wall.

Jack felt his adrenaline building. He was thinking, *Murder-suicide, bad enough, but why take the kids? Were they staying together for the next life?* He took a deep breath, took the disposable camera out of his jacket pocket, and went toward the last room.

Heavy curtains were drawn back. The room was even colder than the rest of the apartment. The master bedroom was spacious enough so that the bodies didn't seem to take up much room in it. A woman and two children lay on a large bed. A man was slumped over on a settee. Jack took a photo of the area, then three more individual shots as he approached the bed. He observed a bottle of NyQuil on one of the two night tables.

The Chinese woman lay on her right side, her left arm

draped across the bodies of the two boys. They were supine, their arms at their sides, dressed in school uniforms. The three of them looked as if they were asleep.

In the far corner of the room were two large red ceramic bowls with dragon designs on them, strategically placed. Jack saw ashes in both. He leaned in closer and took some head shots of the victims.

The woman's eyes were sunken and shadowed. She'd been crying for a long while. She'd dressed conservatively in slacks and sweater top. Jack guessed she was in her mid thirties. Over on the settee, the man was hunched, head down, his open eyes staring at the carpet. He had vomited. He appeared to be in his early forties.

The vomit was dark colored, and Jack guessed from the crust that had formed that it had dried for at least a day.

Opposite the body was a large Chinese armoire that blocked off a neat home-office area: desktop with computers, a printer, and a set of filing cabinets. On top of the cabinets was a stack of books. One was entitled *The Day Trader's Bible.*

Jack used up the rest of his film, taking shots from different angles. He believed photos were a more efficient way to preserve his impressions than written notes and he wanted to take them himself before the crime scene became crowded with the coroner's people and the crime-scene team.

When he was in Chinatown, Jack would drop the camera off at Ah Fook's Thirty-Minute Photo, and Fook Jr. would develop his order first while he went next door to the Mei Wah, got a *nai cha* tea, and watched the gangboys roll by.

He dropped the disposable camera back into his pocket.

Outside the bedroom, Wong said, "Sarge notified the ME

about twenty minutes ago. They're en route in the meat wagon."

"Okay," Jack nodded. He knew Wong wasn't being crude and insensitive. It was just cop talk, jargon they used to take some of the edge off of a traumatic event.

Wong moved toward the main door and the old woman, who was now weeping quietly. Jack went to the window wall of the living room. The view swept north toward the Empire State Building and the jumbled rooftops and billboards of the big city beyond.

The streets below were bustling, a tangle of pedestrian traffic crowding the intersection. The city was in a holiday season rush, and people poured out of the subways and buses, jamming the streets in every direction.

The world goes on, Jack thought. *An entire family offered up to the gods, gods of greed and desire, and the world stops not one second for condolences. Too bad.*

It wasn't the first time Jack had seen dead children, but it was the first time he'd witnessed the end of an entire family. That they happened to be Chinese brought it closer to home, as he assumed it did for P.O. Wong. But as cops they instinctively protected themselves.

Cops got paid to sop up the daily horrors and bloody atrocities that the white-collar suits and ties didn't want to deal with. Cops became hard-hearted, kept a professional distance from the victims, and worked in a way that didn't affect them emotionally. Deeper involvement was a real danger that could lead to overzealousness. Frontline cops became numb to the daily onslaught of unspeakable crimes that crossed the desk blotter day and night. Fifty thousand arrests a year. In a city where teenage mothers disposed of their babies in the garbage, parents were known to kill their children and themselves out of anger, depression, desperation, very often in the grip of an alcohol-and-drug-induced rage.

The Taiwanese, like other Chinese, were obsessed with success and money. The present tragedy was the result of depression over the imminent loss of a certain lifestyle, but it was as much about shame, about *losing face.* Ma's Buddhist beliefs came back to him: *greed and desire.* The Buddhists taught that wanting and having, the material world, could only lead to unhappiness. Life was suffering, and suffering came from desire, the desire for things, for hopes unfulfilled. *Eliminate desire,* and you will eliminate suffering.

Suicide was not uncommon in America, Jack knew. Most were men, and they shot themselves. Then there were drug overdoses, risks taken to disguise a death wish, and, finally, assisted suicide from those who believed in the right to die.

At the apartment door, Jack saw the ends of the packing tape that had been used to secure a quilt over the door so none of the carbon monoxide could escape.

Eliminate desire.

He left Wong at the scene and went down to get a statement from the building manager. He knew the follow-up paperwork at the precinct, plus the reports from the coroner's office, the notification of next of kin, the certificates from the funeral parlor, everything, would take up his next few shifts.

Finally, after sixteen hours on the job, with weariness pulling at his eyelids, he called for a Chinatown *see gay,* car service.

* * *

The Chinese driver spoke Cantonese, and took him straight out to Sunset Park, Brooklyn's Chinatown, without asking directions. Exhausted, Jack powered down the window and let the icy wind slap him awake.

He'd been thirsty long before he reached his studio apartment, but once inside he went directly to the cupboard in the kitchenette, took out a few sticks of incense, and lit them. He shook off the ash and fanned the wiggling tails of smoke as he planted them at the little shrine he'd made for Pa on the Parsons table near the windowsill, where he'd placed an old photo of his father dressed in Chinese-styled *tong jong* clothing.

Pa was now seven weeks buried in the hard ground of Evergreen Hills.

Jack's next visit to the cemetery wouldn't be until mid-January, on what would have been Pa's birthday.

This sad day reminded Jack that he, too, though only twenty-seven, was at the end of his bloodline, a solitary remnant of the Yu clan, whose ancestry retreated back through the generations.

Eighty-eighth cop of Chinese-American descent. A lucky number, he'd thought. But it hadn't worked out that way.

He could still hear the old man's words. "*Chaai lo ah?* Now you're a cop?" Pa had said with derision when Jack first put on the blue uniform. "Chinese don't become policemen. They're worse than the crooks. Everyone knows they take money. *Nei cheega,* you're crazy. You have lost your *jook-sing—* American-born—mind. I didn't raise you to be a *kai dai*—punk idiot—so they can use you against your own people."

I never took any money, Jack hadn't found the chance to say to his father.

16

Jack bowed three times before the shrine, then quickly found the Johnnie Walker Black and poured a tumbler full, cracking open a can of beer to chase it.

The whiskey had only coated his throat with fire. He told himself that the beer would chill him out, would let him sleep better, as he drained the can. He'd lost any appetite he'd had at the crime scene. Now he sat on the edge of his convertible couch nestled in the far corner of the studio. He kicked off his shoes, trying to focus, to make some sense of the days and weeks gone by since Pa's death.

Four months earlier, what began as a hardship transfer to Chinatown's Fifth Precinct to be closer to his dying father, had ended up with a promotion. Then he'd been transferred to the Ninth.

Bad memories from the period in between twisted together as the alcohol reached his brain. He drew the blinds against the afternoon light.

When he closed his eyes, his mind drifted. He fell asleep on the couch.

His sleep was pervaded by a restless disconnected feeling, fitful, punctuated by dreams.

He was seventeen again, running across rooftops at twilight, with Tat Louie, and Wing Lee. Three bloodbrothers, *hingdaai.* Tat was throwing pebbles at the tenement windows and they were shrieking with juvenile laughter as they ran; three Chinatown boys, mad with mischief, having the time of their young lives. Then suddenly, there were the ugly, sneering faces of Wah Ying street-gang members, wielding nasty 007 knives. A swirl of images: Tat, fighting, and Wing, being stabbed. For himself, a quick blackness as he was smashed across his forehead, blood running into his eyes. Then the scene faded to a Chinatown funeral parlor. Wing in a casket, his face dead white, and Tat running out, past the pallbearers, followed by the wailing of Wing's mother. The incense smell of death.

He was watching his youth flash by, viewing it like a camcorder tape, the pictures harsh, unforgiving. Suddenly, Chinese cursing from somewhere, a sound he's heard before. Pa's voice.

Jack felt his body quake uncontrollably. The images flashed in his brain like sparks from a live wire. Japanese soldiers charging forward, samurai swords raised, hacking at Chinese babies, lunging at Chinese women with their bayonets, raping them. The flag with the red Rising Sun fluttering violently in the gale. Butchery. A thousand Chinese heads bouncing and rolling down a blood-slicked slope. And he is sliding, falling.

But this is *Pa's* nightmare.

There is nonstop screaming and yelling, *Say yup poon jai!* Pa cursing, *Jap bastards!* Jack is at Pa's side then, punching away at the bayonets and swords, until he bolts upright on the couch, nearly kicking over the boom-box radio, slowly realizing that it's his own voice barking into the shadowy dark of the small room.

He sat up for a while, caught his breath, and after downing another shot of Johnnie Walker Black, gradually fell back to sleep.

The final dream was short, a twisted vision of Tat, a Chinatown gangster in a black leather trench. Tat "Lucky" Louie, offering him a big bag of money which he didn't accept. Tat, who'd become an ugly liability.

The sound of wind chimes.

Tat has a nine-millimeter strapped to his hip, with sneering street punks spread out behind him. Jack sees his gold police shield dangling from a 007 knife.

He's reaching to block the blade, to retrieve his shield, when darkness finally puts him down for the count.

Dog Eat Dog

Lucky gave the nine-millimeter Smith & Wesson a quick wipe along his shirt sleeve, slipped the clip back in, and chambered a hollow-point round. He flicked down the safety with his thumb and put the spare clip into the side pocket of his black leather blazer, which was draped over the recliner. His attention locked onto the television where Fukienese Chinese demonstrators marched across the big color screen, yelling and carrying signs as they surrounded One Police Plaza.

Lucky sucked back the last of the sensimilla joint, held the smoke a moment, hissed it all out. Then he closed his eyes and thought about *face*, and the future. As *dailo*—boss—of the powerful Ghost Legion gang, he knew that without face, there was no future. He knew intuitively that changes were occurring in his piece of the underworld, especially since the murder of Chinatown's Hip Ching tong godfather, Uncle Four. For the younger Hip Chings, the subsequent death of Golo, Uncle Four's dreaded enforcer, signaled a movement in the ranks. Ambitious heads hinted that the old leadership was ineffectual, and that the organization should be looking toward China-based alliances with outside forces like the triad *Hung Huen,* the Red Circle, alliances with triad paramilitary connections in the south of China. These alliances would bring them AK-47s and grenades. But with a hundred thousand Fukienese on the other side of East Broadway, Lucky felt this might not be a good thing. It might upset the balance of power.

On the TV, the five thousand Fukienese demonstrators were screaming for justice, protesting the shooting death of a Fukienese woman by a gang of teenaged thugs.

A trio of black and Latino teenagers had shot and killed a Chinese woman in a botched robbery of a 99-cent store.

Lucky thumbed down the volume and slipped the Smith & Wesson into a large gun pocket that Ah Wong the tailor had sewn inside his leather jacket. The newcomers to Chinatown, the Fukienese, were trying to gain control, to take over from the established tongs, the On Yee and the Hip Ching. Everyone was looking toward China now and the Fukienese—the Fuk Chings—were leading the way.

The earlier wave of immigrants had come from Canton, now known as Guangzhou, and had spoken Cantonese, as did their brethren from Hong Kong. They couldn't understand the dialect of the recent Fukienese arrivals, who formed their own gangs—the Fuk Chow and Fuk Ching—that respected no one. They recruited only from the desperate dregs of their community.

Power was shifting. On *his* turf, the main strongholds of Chinatown, Fat Lily's massage joint, and Number Seventeen card house, had both been raided in the same week. The cops had come from outside the precinct, in blue windbreakers, under the direction of some unknown Major-Case task force. Someone was feeding them information, directing *gwailo* white cops toward Ghost Legion operations. Could be the Fuks, or maybe double-dealing by one of the other tongs. And his informants in the Fifth Precinct were all gone now. Lucky thought instantly of Jack Yu, *Jacky Boy*, the Chinese cop, the hero cop, his Chinatown homeboy from back in the day. Then he slowly shook his head, with a smile that mixed disdain and annoyance. *Jacky Boy's not in the Fifth, anymore; gone fishing somewhere else in cop world.*

Lucky saw other ominous signs on the horizon. The incoming mayor was a law-and-order guy, an ex-DA who'd already stated publicly that he was going to crack down on organized crime. In the past that had meant the Mafia, Sicilian guys, but now included the Russian *mafiya*, the Mexicans, the city's drug gangs, and the Chinese tongs as well.

Lucky knew to go with the flow, to roll with the blow, but he'd have to be nimble, and make the secret deals that would protect and expand his empire. He'd work out whisper deals with pro-China groups, and even with gangbangers like the Fuk Chings. The Red Circle triad, which partnered with the On Yee and had historical underworld connections to that tong, couldn't be trusted. They were masters of the double-cross. Keep it all close to the vest, he figured, because if the other Ghost factions found out, they might think he was selling them out, getting ready to bail.

One thing was clear: it was all over for the On Yee. Their ties were mostly with Hong Kong and Taiwan. China itself was a whole different ballgame and the Fukienese already had tight connections with corrupt mainland government officials and were rumored to have deserters from the People's Liberation Army on their payroll.

The television news program segued from Fukienese protest to Thanksgiving pageantry. Seeing the Macy's Parade roll across the screen reminded Lucky of his father, Thanksgiving Day being the birthday of the old abusive drunk whom he hadn't seen in five years, the last time being a chance encounter on a Flushing Chinatown street when the sad loser shamelessly asked for a handout. *The fuckin' bum,* thought Lucky, the reason why his mother had run out on them before his teenage years. He wondered if the son of a bitch was still alive, then decided he didn't care.

Disgusted, he punched off the TV.

When Lucky appraised himself in the mirror he still saw a street warrior, but too much Chinatown fast food, beer, and brandy had turned his gut to flab, made him appear bearlike and lumbering.

He checked his Oyster Rolex. It was 9 PM. He glanced toward the darkness of the November night outside his Bayard Street condominium. The wind gusted and banged against the windows. It was freezing outside and he knew most of the Ghost Legion streetboys would be wearing their dark down-filled jackets, puffy enough to hide their guns. He himself, as *dailo,* would only wear the black leather blazer, which made him appear oblivious to the cold, more macho than the others.

Condensation formed at the bottom of the metal window frame, and the spoon-sized thermometer outside the glass read nine degrees. It was almost time to cruise through his rounds, to check on his empire.

Outside the window the streets of the Bowery were empty. At the street corner six flights below, the traffic light, swaying and swinging at the end of the long metal arm that hung over the intersection, was frozen on red. A bus proceeded cautiously through the intersection, rolling north along the Bowery. There was not one person on the frigid streets beneath the dim yellow street lamps.

He could see the Manhattan Bridge, in the darkness looking like a black ribbon suspended from two parallel strands of pearls, arching across the East River toward the Brooklyn waterfront, the Brooklyn Navy Yard.

Two car-horn blasts from directly below broke his reverie. A black car pulled smoothly up to the curb, its white headlights momentarily lighting up the front of the Rickshaw Brother's garage. He pictured Lefty behind the wheel, all spiky haircut and gel, with Kongo, the big dark Malay, riding shotgun by his side. The headlights went to black and the Buick sat like a water bug squatting beside the curb.

Lucky crushed the burnt marijuana roach into a glass dish. He lifted the leather blazer off the recliner, and felt its heft as he slipped it on. Normally, he would not carry the Smith & Wesson, but tonight, going out to the Chinatown fringe at East Broadway, he followed his instincts, and assured himself he was not being paranoid. *Better strapped than sorry.* He turned off the lights and the TV and closed the red door of his condo, took the stairs down, and felt the weight of the pistol in his jacket pocket. Thinking about Fukienese East Broadway, and about how easily power could shift, he went down toward the dark Chinatown street, and the black Buick at the curb.

HENRY CHANG

Black Car, Black Night

The black Buick was a 1988 Riviera, a beefed-up muscle car straight out of Detroit, a wide-body chassis fitted with a thick set of Pirelli tires, and dark-tinted windows. The Riviera had 44,000 miles on it when the Ghosts took it as payment from a gambler who'd lost it in a fan-tan game down one of the basements. Its finish was fading but underneath the hood, a 3600 V6 engine was still capable of churning out a catlike acceleration. The wide tires made it a perfect car for narrow Chinatown streets with corners that were tight and uneven. With Lefty driving, the black car rolled low to the ground and bit into the curves even at a high speed. The car had four-wheel independent suspension and traction control. It sprinted from zero to sixty in six seconds and it could cruise at eighty, and still have enough horsepower for passing in heavy traffic. In the inner city the car was good to go for getaways and drive-bys. It could leap into a sprint and cornered better than the Firebirds and Camaros. Nothing the cops drove could touch it, their standard Dodge cars, running on the cheap gas of a tight-fisted city budget, were too weak.

Lucky had had steel diamond-plate sheets inserted into the door panels, courtesy of Chin Ho Auto Body Repair, in exchange for not making the monthly "contribution" payment. Lefty's cousin Hom Mo, the mechanic at Victor's Fix-Rite garage, kept the engine purring and made sure the oil was fresh.

It was nine after nine when Lucky slid into the backseat of the Riviera.

Lefty fired up the headlights and urged the car away from

24

the curb. They took the backstreets out to Centre Street, then rolled north toward Walker. Lucky never said a word, watching the night go by behind the shadowy mass of Kongo. Lefty knew the first stop was always at Willie Eyeballs, to pick up cash and cigarettes. Willie Wong had eyeballs that bulged, a condition that made him look like a bugged-out horny lecher. An On Yee henchman, he ran a warehouse on Walker Street that stored a thousand cartons of counterfeit cigarettes. Fake Marlboros and Camels, made in China, became part of the flood of untaxed cigarettes into the city that occurred after state taxes went up. The fakes were half the price, and the real butts from out of state were even cheaper. One container load of fakes, fifty thousand cartons, arrived on the docks every month, and two truckloads of tax-frees from down south arrived every other day. The operation sucked in a hundred thousand a week.

The cigarettes went from a container port in Queens to places like Eyeballs's warehouse, out to stores on Canal Street, and in Chinatown, spreading through the Lower East Side and out to the five boroughs and into New Jersey. It was a multimillion-dollar operation run by south China elements of the Red Circle triad partnered with the On Yee tong in New York City.

The Ghosts provided protection for the warehouse and received cash and cases of knock-off smokes in return.

Willie came up to the car shivering, careful to let Kongo see his hands at all times. He handed over an envelope with the five hundred weekly, and a large plastic bag full of cartons of fake Marlboros, complimentary cigarettes for the high rollers in the Ghosts' gambling basements along Mott Street.

The frigid air streaked in as Lucky powered shut the window, watching Eyeballs scurry back into the warehouse.

"Stop by Mimi's," he told Lefty.

They continued north, the streets still empty except for a few factory ladies shivering and sloshing their way down into the subway entrance. Lucky leaned back, watched the nighttime neon colors blur by and considered the rash of robberies of On Yee businesses at the far fringe of Chinatown. Out there at Pike, Allen, other streets adjoining East Broadway. Complaints had been coming in from On Yee merchants. After all, they paid for the protection already, *what the fuck was going on?*

Lee Watch Distribution, a local supplier with a shop on Orchard Street, was part of Skinny Chin's operation that brought in high-end Hong Kong watches bypassing customs. Someone had gotten in and out and took a hundred thousand worth of Rados, Movados, Cartiers, and Rolexes. Skinny was crazed because there was no forced entry, no way in or out except for a tiny bathroom window, too small for anyone to get through.

What am I, a fuckin' detective? Lucky thought, sardonically. But he knew his face, his honor, was at stake.

Since he was a relative of the On Yee treasurer, Skinny's pitching a bitch was sure to make Lucky lose face.

Fuck *that,* and fuck *him,* too, thought Lucky.

The next robbery hit had been at the Jung Wah warehouse on Allen Street, cleaned out of a hundred cases of canned abalone *bao yee,* and a half ton of dried bird's nest, expensive delicacies all. *Who cuts out with a hundred cases and no one sees or hears anything?* Another hundred thousand ripoff. Once again, no forced entry. *Inside job, yo?*

Nothing made sense.

Broome Street came up and they rolled to a stop in front of a shuttered storefront with an awning that read Wholesale

Fashions Inc. Lucky knew the basement contained a quarter-million worth of fake designer handbags, Gucci, Louis Vuitton, Prada, Chanel. Knock-off Nike sweatsuits and bogus Tiffany jewelry. All made in China. Thousand-dollar handbags selling for eighty-eight bucks.

Lefty punched the horn twice and the front door cracked open. A girl with a rice-bowl haircut peeked out, then stepped toward them carrying a shopping bag in each hand. Some kind of Asian, Lucky couldn't tell which, she was petite and wrapped in an oversized down coat. She smiled and handed over the bags through his window. He returned her smile and checked the items as she went back inside. There were three each of the Vuitton and the Prada bags, gifts for his favorite whores at Fat Lily's and Flavio's. And three fake Tiffany tennis bracelets; more gifts to express his extravagance when Christmas rolled around. *Trademark, what fuckin' trademark?*

"Kenmare, then Chrystie," he said to Lefty.

The black car came to a garage and pulled in. The garage was on the block of Kenmare before the street changed to Delancey. It was a half-mile walk from the heart of Chinatown at Mott and Bayard. Kongo stepped out and stood away from the car, let the scattergun slide down into his right hand. Lefty tapped the horn once, and killed the headlights.

A side door of the garage opened and a short Chinese man came out with a sack in his hand. He took one look at Kongo with the scattergun, and slowly placed the sack on the hood of the Riviera before turning and stepping back inside the garage. Kongo took the sack as Lefty backed the car out, and swung it wide, then Kongo climbed in. They drove toward Chrystie.

There were a thousand Ecstasy tablets in the sack, Lucky

knew, and the count was sure to be good. The pills were the result of a handshake deal between the Montreal Ghosts and the Vietnamese crew that manufactured the "club drugs" in Canada. The Vietnamese got the raw materials from The Netherlands and operated several Ecstasy mills in Montreal, Toronto, and Edmonton. The Ghost Legion handled the mules and a million pills a month were smuggled south across the border into the states, winding up in nightclubs and dance-halls across the country. Kongo stashed the sack inside a hidden compartment behind the stick-shift panel. The thousand tablets wouldn't last two weekends in NYC.

They came to a red light and a police cruiser passed in the opposite direction. Lucky felt for the butt of his pistol, but as the police car faded in the rearview mirror, he turned his thoughts back to the robberies out past East Broadway. The USA Garments factory had had its payroll ripped off by armed masked intruders who never uttered a word but instead, communicated with hand signals and signs. Fifty gees *cash.*

Fuk Ching gangbangers? The Dragons again? It didn't seem like their style, and Lucky didn't think they were smart enough anyway. *More than one crew working no-man's-land?* He thought about Koo Jai and the Ghost Legion crew out on East Broadway, farthest from the center. It was Koo Jai's responsibility to control things out there, even though they'd banged up against some Fuk Ching lowboys and were now operating on disputed turf under an unspoken, unofficial truce. *Koo Jai, the pretty-boy hustler with the short pal, Eddie Ng, the stupid Jung brothers, and a few other kids who used to be called the Stars, or something corny like that.*

Lucky would need to call in Koo Jai for a sit-down after the transfers at the gambling basements, and after the whorehouse on Chrystie, toward which Lefty was now turning the dark car.

Chao's

Chao's was a cathouse in a renovated five-story condo building on a quiet part of Chrystie Street near the old junkie park. Lucky brought along one of the Prada bags and dropped a fistful of Ecstasy pills inside it.

Angelina Chao, fortyish, a one-time Hong Kong hostess, ran the tidy little show out of her two-bedroom suite on the fifth floor, with a balcony that looked out over the park and the jumbled maze of rooftops in the distance. Angelina rotated a posse of Asian pussy from Miami, Los Angeles, Las Vegas, and New Orleans.

Appetizers, blowjobs, were fifty bucks a pop.

Chaos, mused Lucky, playing the thought off of Angelina's last name. He had called ahead to Angelina and she'd assured him he'd be the new girl's first suck off of the night. Earlier, he had heard some out-of-town gamblers laughing about a *jop-jung* mixed-breed girl, a *fresh* one over at Angelina's, a half-Cuban half-Chinese *ho* who performed something called a "yingyang" or "blackout" blowjob. Some johns had actually passed out. *What? She knew how to squeeze a john's balls just right, at just the right moment while she was sucking the head so that the juices exploded out as she drained it dry.*

He considered wearing a condom, and saw himself as testing the new merchandise, seeing what the girl's skills were, sort of like quality control.

Lefty and Kongo waited in the car, patiently aware that the basements on Mott Street would be the next stop.

Lucky didn't see any johns hanging around and Angelina waved him into one of the bedrooms. There was a twin bed, a nightstand, and a chair in one corner. The bedspread, the carpet, the curtains, were all red.

He stood by the door and rebuckled his belt after running it through the loop handle of the Prada bag. He swallowed an Ecstasy and waited. After a few minutes the *jop-jung* girl came in through a connecting door. She saw the Prada bag dangling in front of Lucky's crotch and smiled. When she let her red silk gown slip off her shoulders, Lucky saw she was naked, a bodacious tanned body with an exotic face that displayed the best of her two bloodlines. Feline brown eyes and lips that were puffy, swollen, and sexy. Long silky black hair that shimmered when she turned her face.

She knelt down before him and unbuckled his belt, carefully placing the Prada bag to one side, never taking her eyes off him even as she unzipped his fly. She tugged down his pants, and pulled his *lun* cock out, caressing it with her French-tip fingernails.

"*Dios mio,*" she exclaimed softly, "*Nei dai sai.*" My god, how big you are, playing him along in two languages.

"*Nei ho yeh,*" he answered sarcastically. "*You're the winner.* I heard you're the best."

She smiled again, licked her lips, and then ran her tongue in a circle around the head of his cock. She licked it until it was swollen, and proceeded to suck him slow and strong.

The Ecstasy was working against the *sensimilla* now, working him like a yo-yo.

He felt the strength draining from his arms, his legs, all his blood rushing toward his cock, his heart pumping hard to keep things working. The shortness of breath caught him as he saw the mass of shiny black hair bobbing up and down at his stomach. She tightened her lips and deep-throated him. The pressure was building in his head, ready now. She was stroking his shaft, caressing his balls with her other hand. His orgasm exploded into her mouth, four, five, six loads. The noise he heard was his own groaning, the sweet anguish throbbing in his loins.

He was sucking in air through his nostrils, his mouth gasping like a fish, his thighs quivering as he braced his back against the door. He let his heart slow down as he came back to earth. When she turned her head he saw a sweet face, contemplating her palms. She looked up at him with her big brown eyes, then opened her mouth, and tilted her head to let the thick milky jism spill over her lower lip, her tongue pushing the spittle and saliva out into her palms. A thick translucent strand clung to her chin. She smiled and wiped it off with the back of her hand. Reaching into the nightstand, she took out a small towelette and wiped the stickiness off his shaft. There was no need for words and he watched her as she turned, still on all fours, crawling her way off with the red gown and the Prada bag in tow, giving him a rear view of her departing pussy. She stood up at the connecting door, and their eyes met a last time before she exited the room. *China-cubana.*

He took a deep breath, pulled his pants up, zipped his fly, and after a few shaky steps, made his way back to the frozen night and the black car.

*   *   *

It was a short ride back from Chrystie to Mott Street, so Lucky left the window open, the cold wind on his face working with the Ecstasy, refocusing his mind.

The On Yee always collected cash off the streets before holiday weekends, and squared up the Chinese accounts, before the crush of waiters crowded into the gambling dens, their pockets fat with Thanksgiving Dinner tip money from the *gwailo* white devils.

When they reached Bayard Street, it was almost ten-thirty, early yet for the gambling crowd. Lefty parked the Riviera on Mulberry, facing north, and out, toward the Holland Tunnel or the Manhattan Bridge, a quick left or right if they needed to bust out of Chinatown.

Lucky, Lefty, and Kongo walked onto Mott and the street was quiet except for the shrill whistle of the arctic wind.

They went into Number Nine basement first.

The basement was brightly lit, and Lucky saw one mahjong game underway, but otherwise there was only a smattering of the association's cronies hanging around making lowball bets just to keep the action going. It was cold out, and anyway, the night was young for the night crawlers, he thought.

Kongo gave the fake Marlboros to the house manager and stood to one side, overlooking the one active table of thirteen-card poker. There were no players at the fan-tan or *paigow* tables, and the dealers were smoking cigarettes, drinking coffee, and watching Chinese cable television. Lefty took the Ecstasy pills over to Number Sixty-Six basement, where other Ghosts would package them into small plastic baggies before delivery to local karaoke joints and uptown discos and dance clubs.

Lucky dropped another hit of Ecstasy, and then chased it with a shot of Johnnie Black. He waited as the managers tallied their accounts. The players would show up soon enough so the basements would be jammed again, and he still wanted to place a hot bet with the Chinese bookie at the OTB, but the troubles out at East Broadway kept bouncing to the front of his mind and crowded out the images of blowjobs and bodacious bodies. Instead, he saw a crew of incompetent Ghosts, thought about Koo Jai—Kid Koo—and called his pager. Lefty came back with a suitcase of cash for the manager and turned it over to the house accountants. Then he swallowed an Ecstasy and stood next to Kongo by the door, watching the house take money off the card table.

Lucky watched them all, but he was feeling impatient, thinking about *face*, and the far end of East Broadway.

OTB

The Chinatown OTB branch was the highest performing betting parlor on the Lower East Side, grossing a hundred thousand a day, while serving the biggest volume of gamblers in the city. That volume did not include the large number of Chinese gamblers who placed their bets with the Chinese bookies working the streets outside the OTB.

The average Chinese gambler, who didn't speak much English other than the name of the horse and maybe the track where the race would be held, preferred the services of the Chinese bookies. These bookies offered a 10-percent discount on bets of ten dollars or more, and unlike OTB, did not require that a W2-G tax form be completed, and a driver's license and a social security card be provided for winnings above six hundred dollars.

No illegal Chinese, no *prudent* Chinese, was going to furnish that information, especially since many of the old-timers placed exotic bets that were more difficult to win, but which would generally pay out more than six hundred.

Fong *Sai Go*—fourth brother Fong—considered himself a bookmaker, *johng ga,* but in reality he was only a *teng jai,* a small sampan, in the vast ocean of illegal Chinese gambling. He was a small-time Chinatown bookie, sanctioned to work the main OTB by his village association cronies who owned the building from which the OTB operated. The other family associations went along, and the tongs didn't make a fuss as long as they got their piece of the action.

Sai Go held the gold-plated metal card in his hand, running his thumbnail over the dragon and the Goddess of Mercy etchings, over the Chinese words on either side of this Buddhist talisman, a gold credit card–sized panel of metal featuring laser-etched phrases: *cheut yop ping on,* or "peace be with you," and "a safe journey always." He began to consider the irony of how the *bot gwa,* talisman, had failed him, when he noticed the front end of the betting floor filling up, the frigid cold outside driving indoors the throng of Chinese waiters and kitchen staff just come off the late shift.

Sai Go stood off to one side, where he had a good view of the wide-frame color television monitors showcasing holiday horse racing from Golden Gate, Los Alamitos, Delta Downs. The overseas action from Down Under—Sydney, Melbourne, Caulfield—would come later, but in Hong Kong, races from the Happy Valley track, and from the Sha Tin oval in China, were getting ready to be run.

He put away the talisman and saw that it was well after midnight. A few more gamblers came in and joined the noisy smelly mix of men in *meen nop* cotton-padded vests and down jackets shaded gray, brown, black—the somber tones of the working class. There was the faint burnt smell of dead cigarettes on the sticky linoleum covering the floor.

A crew of young Chinatown gangbangers came in, wearing black down coats and punky haircuts. Several wore black racing gloves with the fingers cut off. They fanned out through the betting parlor, and Sai Go instinctively brushed his hand back to feel for the box-cutter steel in his rear pocket. He felt better when he saw Lucky, the *dailo,* step into the room with another crew of Ghosts.

Lucky spotted him immediately, went in his direction. The crowd parted for the dark phalanx that escorted him, eight crazies and a big dark-skinned Malay.

Sai Go thought about the pad in his pocket as the crew came to the back of the house. He decided not to reach into his jacket as they circled him.

"I want a thousand on Ming Sing, to win," said Lucky, "in the second race at Happy Valley."

"Ming Sing," Sai Go repeated, acknowledging the bet.

"Any action on that yet?" from Lucky.

"You're the first," Sai Go answered, waiting for his moment to change the subject.

Lucky had overheard one of the uncles explaining how the fix was in, and how Ming Sing, *movie star,* a three-year-old gelding from Australia, was an eight-to-one payout. Lucky didn't catch the details but figured that the Hong Kong triads had probably kidnapped a family member or relative of a jockey, or trainer, and maybe paid off or coerced other jockeys to hold back or block out for the "fixed" winner.

Lucky didn't stress any of that, or the big bet, win or lose. He was putting back into play the fifteen-hundred winnings he'd just taken out of the Mott Street basements.

Sai Go said, "You can catch it on the satellite channel . . ."

Lucky already knew that, but held his eyes on Sai Go while firing up a Marlboro.

"So what's this problem you have? Lucky asked, exhaling smoke. "One of the boyz owes you money?" He could see that Sai Go was relieved, appreciative that the gang leader was addressing the situation.

"It's that kid, he's about your height. *Leng jai,* a good-looking kid. They call him Koo, or cool, something like that."

Lucky was careful to downplay his own curiosity. "But how come you gave him that much play?" Lucky said, more an admonishment than a question.

"He bet a few times before this," Sai Go countered. "And he always had money. A few thousand was no problem."

Lucky blew out the cigarette smoke in a tight stream. "A few thousand walking-around cash, huh?"

"Correct," answered Sai Go.

Both men were quiet a long moment. Sai Go spoke first.

"It's just that he said he wasn't going to pay me. In front of all the bettors. He didn't give me any face to work with, and—"

"I'll take care of it," Lucky interrupted, *"gau dim,* done. You said a thousand, right?"

"Correct again, *dailo,"* said Sai Go, bowing slightly. Now he felt his blood pressure rising, tension starting to grab in his forehead.

Lucky jerked his head at the big Malay, flicked his Marlboro to the linoleum, and crushed it under his heel. The others made a path for him and they went back through the crowd.

Sai Go watched them leave as he penciled Lucky's bet onto his pad of soluble tissue sheets. He could swallow the paper anytime and evidence of betting records would dissolve before reaching his stomach. There was a flash of dizziness and then he felt short of breath. *It's the medication,* he thought, *the* gwailo *white devil medicine that was supposed to cure even the worse of all diseases.*

One of his cell phones blared a musical tune, and he readied his betting pad. It was Big Fat, calling in bets from the China Garden. In Sai Go's peripheral view the ponies were thundering across the big color monitors. He was feeling lightheaded as he jotted down numbers next to the nickname Big Fat. He knew all his players by their nicknames. *Pai Kwut* was Spare Ribs. *Gee Jai,* Little Pig. All of them like that. The others would be calling in soon.

Hang in there, he thought, *it's just the medication.* He felt the need for some cold night air, and slowly made his way toward the shivering bodies at the front vestibule.

On the Edge

Out at the end of East Broadway, past the lumberyard and the old synagogue, where it crossed Essex Street, stood the 1-6-8 Bar, formerly called the Mickey Rose, a one-time Irish whiskey joint that was supposedly affiliated with the Campisi crew from the Knickerbocker Houses. It was two blocks from the Rutgers Projects, and a block east of Saint Teresa's Church, more than a half mile from Mott Street.

The big white fluorescent sign above the bar was the only light around the dark deserted intersection. The design on the sign spelled out BAR with the numbers one, six, and eight crowding a cocktail glass tilted at an angle.

Inside, the room was long and narrow, dimly lit by a row of blue lights suspended from the ceiling. There was a twenty-foot wooden bar counter on the left, with a dozen bar stools, and a few small tables in the back. On the right side were red plastic booths that ran toward a pool table in the rear.

The customers had changed through the years, and were now mostly people from the housing projects, the Seward Park area, and Chinese gangbangers working the Chinatown fringe. Whites, blacks, Hispanics, and Chinese mixing tenuously together.

It was almost midnight and the only noise came from the crew of Ghosts drinking in the back area by the pool table.

Koo Jai, or Kid Koo, sat in the last booth and took a swig from his Heineken bottle, watching the homey Jung twins and Shorty Ng chase a rack of nine-ball around the table. He was reminiscing about the time back in the old days, when these streets belonged to the Red Stars, long before the Ghost Legion took over, and way before the waves of Fukienese snakeheads that had followed. Now the Fuks, *fucks,* as he called them, were buying up property on the Chinatown frontier, and were running their own rackets, like the mahjong room on Henry Street that in better days would have coughed up a piece of the action to the Stars. Now, everyone who paid protection out here paid to the old Chinatown Cantonese, or to the new Fukienese snakehead organizations. And the Dragons were also claiming disputed territory.

Shorty bopped to the far end of the table, tapping the butt end of his cue stick against the wood floor, sizing up the game-winning shot. Considerably shorter than five feet, he'd need to get on his toes, stretching long across the table, to hit the nine ball right, and not scratch.

An awkward shot no matter.

One of the Jungs cleared his phlegmy throat.

Shorty missed the nine ball, left it as an easy kiss in the corner, a hanger.

The Jungs snickered, snorted.

"Dew gow keuih!" Shorty cursed "Fuckin' ball shit," slapping his palm against the side rail.

Koo Jai smirked, took another swallow of the beer.

"Fuck," Shorty said again, jerking his head as he circled away from the table. Koo Jai threw him a disapproving shake of the head, thinking, *Shorty,* the smallest guy in the gang, but with the biggest attitude. *Superstitious guy.* Wouldn't pull a job on a rainy day, or on any date that had a four in it. Refused to enter a place if it were on the fourth floor, or fourteenth, and so on. Afraid of *death,* which sounded like four in Chinese.

Young Jung pocketed the nine ball hanger, a toothy grin across his face. He sauntered off as Shorty reluctantly stooped to rack up a new game.

Koo Jai closed his eyes a few seconds and suddenly felt a gust of cold wind, looking up to see the dark bulk of Kongo by the open door at the front of the bar. He was even more surprised to see the *dailo* Lucky step through the door, coming toward the pool table.

The banter around the table went quiet.

Outside, a car's horn beeped once. He saw headlight shadows against the door wall flashing to black.

In the next instant, Lucky was in front of him.

"Yo, what the fuck, man?" Lucky said in a steely voice. "I paged you almost an hour ago."

Koo Jai lowered his head slightly, said sheepishly, "Sorry, Boss, the battery must've died."

"Your fuckin' brain must've died." Lucky took the Smith & Wesson out for emphasis, laid it on the rail of the pool table. "What the fuck is going on out here?"

Koo Jai knew this wasn't a social visit, but he seemed genuinely puzzled, trading glances with Shorty and the Jung brothers in the sudden hush. Lucky sneered, turning his hard face toward Koo Jai.

"How come you got nobody on the street? Do you know what's going on out there?" Lucky paused a moment for effect. "KJ, you're the senior brother. Tell me what's going on?" He let his fingers drift over the pistol, waited.

"We're out here watching out for the neighborhood," Koo Jai said evenly, "like we *been* doing, making sure the *hok-kwee* and the *loy sung* don't fuck over the Chinese."

Lucky picked up the gun and said, "You're doing all that by being here in this bar? You're really keeping an eye on things, right? And now you're only pretending to be drinking and shooting pool, right?"

"Check the streets," Koo Jai said quickly to Shorty and the Jungs.

"Hell, it's freezing out there!" groused Shorty as they went toward the front door.

"We were out earlier," explained Koo Jai. "And the streets were empty. It's too fuckin' cold. We only came in to warm up."

Lucky went behind Koo Jai and stood there with the gun.

"I'm telling you," he said, "someone's ripping off company business out here, and it's fuckin' bad for *our* business, 'cause it makes us look bad. I want your guys on the street, their eyes peeping for hijacks, their ears open."

Koo Jai nodded in agreement with the *dailo,* but also said, "It's hard to understand the Fuks. When they talk, it sounds like they're spitting or shitting."

"Whatever," Lucky warned, facing Koo now. "You better get a grip on out here. Because I'm telling you, boy, if there's another rip-off, it's gonna be on you."

"Okay, Boss," said Koo Jai quietly, trying to save face. "But I have a question."

Lucky nodded at him. "Speak."

Koo Jai's voice was firmer now. "You know we're out here dealing with the junkie *hok-kwees,* the niggers, and the PRs, and now, not only do we have to watch out for the Dragons, we got those fuckin' Fuk Ching assholes picking at us, too."

Lucky's eyes narrowed, "What about it?"

"Tell me again," Koo Jai asked, keeping a tone of respect in his voice, "why we're holding back, why we don't just *sot* fuckin' crush them all?"

"Everyone was told to cool it. There are some *arrangements* being worked on, upstairs, with the old men."

Koo Jai understood that to mean the tongs were dealing. He knew better than to question the *dailo,* or the uncles. "Yeah," he said quietly, "but the Fuks spit on Shorty, and Dragons pissed all over Jung's car."

Lucky raised the pistol past Koo Jai's eye level.

"Don't worry about them. When the time's right, we'll clean it all up." Lucky put the pistol back into his gun pocket, clenched his jaw, and checked his Rolex. "Right now, I wanna know who's pulling off these jobs."

"Okay, Boss," Koo Jai said as Lucky headed for the door, with Kongo taking his back.

"Sure thing," he said to himself, as he watched the Mott Street *dailo* exit the seedy East Broadway bar.

Night Without End

When Jack woke again, it was pitch black in the studio apartment, the only light a faint glow of digital numbers on the face of the boom-box radio. It was after 10 PM.

He decided to get dressed, walked down to Eighth Avenue, and wolfed down some Shanghai dumplings with hot sauce at one of the all-night soup shacks. When he was done, it was eleven-thirty and he got into the first Chinese radio car lined up on the street outside, quickly rolling toward the Brooklyn Bridge.

The *see gay* car descended to the Manhattan side, went north on the Bowery heading out of the Fifth and toward the Ninth.

Ninth and Midnight

On his desk were the crime-scene photos of the Chinese family, the Kungs, a file folder, and a note from P.O. Wong. As Jack had requested, Wong had arranged for a Chinatown car service to drive the grandmother home, and in a follow-up phone call, had learned that the family had made burial arrangements with the Heaven Grace Funeral Home in Flushing. The death certificates would be available there.

The next of kin, their worst fears realized, were en route to New York.

The photos brought it back to him, the idea that suicide was not uncommon, but that this case was different. The demise of entire families, especially involving young children, was particularly tragic.

The folders contained the reports from One Astor Plaza. The building manager's narrative was just as Jack had remembered, straightforward, and practically mirroring the security officer's report. They'd all gone up together and discovered the horror at the scene. The reports were standard TPO format: time, place, occurrence.

The Medical Examiner's report on the dead family cited chemical asphyxiation as the cause of death. If the body doesn't receive oxygen, it leads to collapse, coma, and death. *Suffocation*

43

by carbon monoxide. All four bodies showed lethal levels of the invisible odorless poison. The mother and the children also showed large doses of sleep medication, the NyQuil, more than enough to have made them drowsy. The father had no trace of it. *His job was to keep the briquettes burning, to keep the carbon monoxide flowing.* He'd gotten sick during the killing and dying, maybe realizing in his daze the enormity of what he and his wife were doing, frantically knowing it was much too late to turn back.

Jack remembered the photos of the big red dragon bowls. Those bowls had held more charcoal and ashes than the saucepans and pots in the kitchen area.

He closed the file and placed it, along with the photos, back into the wire basket. He remembered Pa's passing and thought about the cycle of events that the survivors would soon have to endure: the funeral home, the wake, the burial, and the church or temple. Later, the return to the cemetery, closure a long way off, if ever.

He began to wrap up the paperwork, drawing together the official loose ends of the case.

P.O. Wong had also left Jack a Post-it note, an unofficial comment at the margin of the reports; Wong intended to go to the Kung family wake, which was in Flushing's Chinatown. *Closure for him,* thought Jack, *a good thing.* Having been touched by death, superstitious Chinese believed paying last respects was a way to close off the bad luck.

The shift dragged on.

Jack checked the blotter, the patrol reports, and the updates on the computer.

In Brooklyn's Seven-Two Precinct a jewelry-store robbery

had turned into a wild chase and a carjacking. Four of the seven armed robbers of the Galleria Gems Center got away. Three perps being held.

In Queens, a fight over a young beauty exploded violently when a teen slashed his roommate and was captured an hour later. The woman involved had no comment.

In the 0-Five, the Chinatown precinct, two gang members had been arrested while awaiting a ransom payment for a kidnapped and tortured Chinese immigrant.

Jack wondered if Tat's Ghosts might be involved, but figured that it was more likely to be a Fukienese setup. The victim and the perps all had mainland Mandarin-sounding names, Zhang instead of Chang, Qiu instead of Chu. In a second Chinatown incident, an unidentified Chinese man had been ambushed by at least two assailants as he left a restaurant and shot numerous times, but was in stable condition at Downtown Hospital. Uniforms from the 0-Five had responded but were unable to get cooperation from area residents or merchants. *No surprise there,* Jack thought. What caught his attention was the unusual heavy-duty firepower involved, rounds not typical of Chinatown violence: .45 caliber, and .223 rifles, hitters strapping AK-47s, Colt .45, and 9mm Parabellums. The victim had apparently shot back with a .38 revolver, a pea shooter by comparison.

Power struggle, mused Jack, *or someone had a nasty beef to settle.*

Out on the edge of the Ninth, the reports had arrived early. Toys "R" Us had held a 7 AM sale where two shoppers were arrested for bashing each other over a ten-dollar talking Spider-Man doll. At Kmart, a riot had broken out, with aggressive shoppers trampling each other to get to a fifty-dollar color TV.

For Giving, *thanks . . .*

P.O.s and cars to the scene.

From Black Friday to the days before Christmas, businesses were marching from loss to profitability. Ads for sales and discounts lured shoppers into the stores and malls, feeding the frenzy of shopping that overwhelmed the moral and spiritual message of the holidays. The thought brought back to Jack one of Ma's Buddhist sayings: *To attain nothingness is true happiness.* The saying flew in the face of capitalism and did not work well in this city, this country, this modern world of money and machines. A belief better left to monks on high mountain steppes, away from the din and roar of industrialized civilizations everywhere.

The way that things flowed, the *tao,* kept him on call, on edge, but even then the Chinatown things crowded back into his head. *The killing of the Ping lady, which had provoked the Fukienese demonstrations, the burglaries, the gang crime and brazen gunplay,* events outside his jurisdiction pecking at his sense of duty.

Old Chinese grandmothers get run over by trucks all the time on Canal Street. They walk too slowly and seem to believe no driver will dare run them down. They are at fault yet these are tragedies nonetheless.

Who really cares?

In a cop's life, the more he touched upon tragedy, the more it rubbed off on him, became part of him. Too much tragedy drove some cops to eating their guns.

Trying to clear the black kharma from his mind, his thoughts came to Alexandra Lee, *activista* lawyer and friend. He remembered that he needed to thank her for her help in arranging his recent Hawaiian vacation. He decided to visit her NoHo office after the shift, but he'd go down to Chinatown first, drop by on Billy Bow, *homeboy,* at the tofu factory.

Approaching meal break, Jack ordered take-out sushi from Avenue B, a trendy joint where you could still get raw fish at 3 AM. Four blocks from the stationhouse, he considered the quick jog to Avenue B and back as exercise, movement of the blood.

EDP Avenue B

The trendy sushi spot was still jamming at three in the morning, full of weekend club crawlers slinking out of dance palaces like Webster Hall and Limelight, the party crowd needing to tone down what remained of the Ecstasy rush with sake and raw fish.

U2 jams kicking off the DJ jukebox.

Jack was paying for his Nabeyaki Special, a soup-and-sushi combo, when he heard a commotion outside, on the street that had been deserted on his way in.

The patrons turned their heads.

The restaurant's manager, a young Asian Pacific dude, who tried to look *yakuza* but who struck Jack as more NYU Business Management School, pushed his way out the door to check out the disturbance.

Pocketing his change, Jack went toward the door.

When he stepped out onto the street he saw a short white

man by the curb, in a fatigue army coat, howling up at the streetlamps beneath the cold black night. His hot breath was a rush of steam in the frozen air. He kept his hands in the coat pockets.

EDP, Jack recognized, emotionally disturbed person.

The restaurant manager, deciding how to approach him, kept at a distance.

"Excuse me, *man,* excuse me," the NYU *yakuza* pleaded.

The *ED* man looked to be in his twenties, homeless, snot dripping off his nose. Looked like a bugged-eyed Charlie Manson.

He continued yelling.

Jack was wondering if any of the neighbors had called 911 yet when the man took a step toward the sushi manager.

You had to be careful with EDPs, remembered Jack; there was no telling how they'd react.

State institutions had dumped thousands of them, and many of these walking timebombs had found their way to the city, which was unprepared to deal with them.

Jack flashed his gold badge, said authoritatively, " Hey, *pal,* how's about we get you into a warm shelter? Get you a hot bowl of soup? A bed?"

He imagined he heard sirens in the distance.

The disturbed man turned toward Jack, and smiled, slowly bringing his hands up to his face. He pulled back the outside corners of his eyes, making slanted *chinky* eyes. Then he laughed, a big howl.

"Ya *Jap* muddafukker!" he screamed at Jack. "You ain't no cop! Ya sneaky cocksucker!" He spat at the Asian manager, who stepped away from Jack.

Okaay, realized Jack, *disturbed,* but not so disturbed that he couldn't dredge up the racism in his soul. The words and curses drove the humanity and compassion out of Jack's heart. He saw the man now as just another deranged skell, a danger to himself, if not others.

The skell dropped down into a kind of Kung Fu stance, making catlike Bruce Lee sounds.

Be cool, Jack thought, taking a step back. The skell's mind might be screwed up, but that didn't mean there was anything wrong with his body.

Suddenly the skell launched himself at Jack.

Instinctively, Jack twisted his hip and leaned back as the wild man's foot whipped up, missing Jack but punting his sushi takeout into the street. The Manson clone's right hand came out of the coat with something metallic, swinging down toward Jack in a wide arc.

Jack threw up a *bow arm* that blocked the attack, and stepped into him, hooking his foot, and throwing him off balance. Jack rocketed a stiff palm into his chest and the skell fell backward, into a dive. After he hit the sidewalk, Jack put a knee in his back and slammed his wrist, sending a box cutter skittering along the sidewalk. The fight went out of him when the cuffs went on. *Crazy,* but not stupid.

Jack caught his breath while the sushi manager profusely thanked him, the *ying hung* hero of the moment. Splattered along the gutter were the udon noodles and the *hamachi.*

Flashing lights from the patrol car less than a half-mile away. Down the avenue, EMS rolling in.

They'd work out the chain of custody, and the EDP would wind up in Bellevue for psych observation. Homeless outreach services would follow. Eventually, he'd be put back on medication and released, another timebomb, back into the population.

There would be future victims.

By the time Jack got it all straightened out with the uniforms he'd lost his appetite, and made his way back to the station-house for the end of the overnight.

White Devil Medicine

Sai Go fingered the switch, and stood in the dim yellow light. He noticed it was past 4 AM as he removed his wristwatch and laid it on the counter of the bathroom sink. When he looked in the mirror, he saw a haggard beat-up old man. He was only fifty-nine. Dead eyes that were sinking into the emaciated face. The gray-white crewcut hairs sprouting out, in need of a trim. The stubble spreading from his chin.

The little plastic bottles were in a line up behind the sliding mirror glass of the medicine cabinet. Although he was proud that he could usually read aloud in his broken English the colorful names assigned to the horses on the racing form, the words on the pill bottles were unfathomable.

Taxol.

They'd found a tumor in his lung. *Nodule. Adenocarcinoma.*

He was finding it hard to stay focused.

Vinorelbin.

One pill twice a day. One pill every two days.

He forgot which was which. The pills had him in a daze.

The red ones with the white stripe, every third day.

The blue ones, *one a day?*

The yellow tablets, the purple capsules . . .

Leukocidin.

Words that were meaningless to him, like small black bugs flitting across the square of prescription notepaper from the clinic. New sounds that rattled in his ears, alien noises.

Gum Sook, the herbalist, told him to stop smoking, and to brew up some tea of Job's tears and brown sugar. *No lizard or bladder or powder of horn or dried bull penis.*

Chemotherapy.

Radiation.

More dancing bugs. He'd lose his hair and be sick a lot.

Chat Choy, the head chef at Tang's Dynasty, advised him to boil three cloves of garlic, eat them with soy sauce. Longshot Lee, senior waiter at the Garden Palace, said with quiet confidence, "Fry three cloves of garlic in olive oil, add black pepper, ginger, and salt with shiitake mushrooms. Twice a day. Two months."

Fifty-nine's too young to die nowadays.

Four months left was not enough time.

Forget all this, he concluded in his exhaustion. *We all die sooner or later.*

I'm not taking any more gwailo *pills.* It was more painful trying to stay alive than to accept dying. His thoughts began to scatter far and wide, somewhere between being high and falling down dizzy. It was all unraveling now. He felt it in his cancer blood, paying for his sins, his life in free fall, spiraling down helpless and hopeless.

He coughed quietly and swallowed, already tasting the blood in his throat. Flicking off the light, he let his eyes adjust and left the bathroom.

The living room was dark, but he turned on the television set and let its light fill the room. He thumbed down the volume and rewound the videotape player to the second race at Happy Valley. On the shelves next to the cable box he'd set up his own little wire room operation, where he charged up his cell phones, kept his pads of soluble paper, and reviewed the odds at different overseas race tracks.

In the glare of electronic light the twenty-year-old living-room set exposed a beat-down convertible sofa bed, matching wood-veneer end tables, and a desk that served as a dining table.

He sat down on the sofa and started the videotape. A sunny day in Hong Kong, but he could see it was a sloppy track. They'd probably had rain in the morning.

The riders, with their colorful silk outfits calmed their mounts as they loaded into the gates. He followed the horses: Gung Ho Warrior, Buddha's Baby, Fool Manchu, Happy Dragon, Sword of Doom, Baby Bok Choy, Noble Emperor, Ming Sing, Chu Chu Chang. Double Happiness, and Secret Asian Man, and Geisha's Gold. A crowded field of twelve.

Suddenly, they were off, breaking from the gates. With the volume off, Sai Go was calling the race in his head, seeing the *fix* with wicked clarity.

At the break, it's Geisha's Gold along the rail, with Noble Emperor challenging for the lead, followed by Buddha's Baby. Fool Manchu and Baby Bok Choy a length back for third. A gap of two, it's Double Happiness, Ming Sing outside him, and Chu Chu Chang, settling in toward the rail, with Secret Asian Man and Happy Dragon chasing them. Gung Ho Warrior drops back, with Sword of Doom bringing up the rear as they pound into the first turn.

It's Geisha's Gold and Noble Emperor chased by Fool Manchu a length back, then a close-packed crowd of Buddha's Baby and Chu Chu Chang in front of Baby Bok Choy, Ming Sing, and Secret Asian Man. Happy Dragon boxed to the rail by Gung Ho Warrior and Double Happiness. In last, Sword of Doom is stalking them all.

Down the backstretch it's still Geisha's Gold and Noble Emperor. Behind them the others are scrambling for position, dropping in, and saving ground, barreling out or breaking sharply, all driving to catch the leader. The pace quickens; Ming Sing is in ninth position. A half mile to go.

Secret Asian Man dances around the outside and takes the lead. Ming Sing is boxed in along the rail in eighth place. The field is bumping and pushing the leaders.

They come to the clubhouse turn.

It's still Secret Asian Man, with Buddha's Baby, and Chu Chu Chang ready to pounce. Ming Sing is in seventh.

They're three-wide off the turn. Double Happiness, Chu Chu Chang, and Buddha's Baby. Ming Sing is sixth, the rest of the field digging for the leaders.

At the top of the stretch, the jockeys are waving their whips.

The leaders spread apart a gap. Ming Sing dodges out and follows Double Happiness down the middle of the track. Sword of Doom, fighting through horses, chases them. Buddha's Baby loses ground, and Chu Chu Chang blocks off the rest of the field.

A mad dash the last three lengths and at the wire it's Ming Sing by a neck, then Double Happiness, and Sword of Doom. Buddha's Baby finishes fourth.

Sai Go pumped his fist and cheered quietly. The race, which

took merely a minute to run, had been a thing of beauty. He waited for the posting of the payout, thinking that his exotic bets, via his man at Happy Valley, were going to bring in more than ten grand. He had taken Lucky's pick, Ming Sing, and boxed the bet with other longshots into double and treble wagers. The exotic bets available in Hong Kong made the same type of action in the states seem like standard play; payouts in the *Fragrant Harbor* were astronomically higher.

He downed a shot of Chivas and sat on the sofa as he waited.

The numbers came up on the screen.

The *dailo* Lucky had won more than six thousand, but Sai Go's own exotic bets had won him over eleven thousand. Minus the *dailo*'s money, his take was over five thousand, all from working a hot fix.

The money would be wired into his U.S. Asia bank account the next day, minus his Happy Valley cohort's commission and the transaction fee.

Sai Go rubbed his eyes and turned off the set, plunging the room into blackness. *What to do?* he wondered. *How to enjoy the jackpot?* when the irony of it all came back upon him.

What was he thinking? With four months to live, he was getting excited about taking five thousand out of Happy Valley? *Should have made a list,* he thought, *of all the Chinaman things to do before cashing in.*

Go to Bangkok, drink, and fuck himself to death.

Go see all the places he'd never been.

Go home to Hong Kong and China to say good-bye to the few elderly relatives who were still on speaking terms with him.

Now, closer to the end of the line, he wasn't sure he wanted to take his death on the road. He considered making his last stand in Chinatown, hunkered down in his rent-controlled one-bedroom walk-up.

He had about twenty-eight thousand in the bank, and a fifty-thousand-dollar life insurance policy from Nationwide that still listed his ex-wife as beneficiary. That was it. No wife, no kids, no family. Parents long since passed. His sister and cousins, all estranged. *World without end, amen.*

He knew he needed to take his money off the street, call in all debts. He could explain, if necessary, that he was starting a bigger operation, and required a larger financial investment. Once he recouped everything, he told himself, he'd still have time left to do whatever it was that one does at the end of one's life.

He thought about getting a haircut, a massage, a Chinese newspaper, but quickly fell asleep on the sofa, in the darkness unsure of where the rest of his life would lead after that.

Roll By

In the rush-hour morning, Jack caught the M103 bus running, almost at St. Mark's. The city bus brought him quickly down to Chinatown. He hopped off near Bayard and went west to Mott Street, past the old tenement where he'd grown up, where Pa had finally died.

A crowd of old folks had gathered, blocking the sidewalk outside Sam Kee Restaurant. Jack crossed the street, away from the dingy storefronts that had seen the better days of his youth.

Billy's tofu factory was down the block. Billy Bow, the only son of an only son, was Jack's oldest neighborhood friend. He had been Jack's extra eyes and ears on the street, and he'd provided Jack with insights and observations into the arcane workings of the old community.

The Tofu King was the work of three generations of a longtime Chinatown family, the Bows. It was once the biggest distributor of tofu products in Chinatown, but was clearly no longer the king. Competition had grown steadily as new immigrants from China arrived, and the Tofu King now resorted to promotional gimmicks to hang on to its customers. Every Tuesday was Tofu Tuesday, half-price for senior citizens, and after 6 PM daily, rice cakes and *dao jeong* soybean milk were three for a dollar.

Billy's grandfather had started it all by growing his own bean sprouts, then perfected the process of cooking soybeans and passed it on to his son, Billy's dad, who then hooked up with soybean farmers in Indiana, and expanded the shop. Finally, Billy, conscripted into the family business, targeted their tofu products toward a more diverse health-oriented marketplace, and expanded the shop into the Tofu King. Now the business struggled, not only to maintain its place against the new competition, but also staggering under myriad business costs that kept rising.

Jack remembered the three rudderless years he'd worked in the Tofu King, in the suffocating backroom, cooking and slopping beans into *foo jook* tofu skins, and tofu *fa* custard. That was long after his pal Wing Lee died, but before Jack had finally graduated from City College.

When he peered through the steamy storefront window, he could see Billy near the back, animated, making faces, and gesturing with his hands.

Jack stepped into the humid shop and listened as Billy ranted on about the latest atrocities. "The *health* department, *wealth* department is what they should call it, comes down with a new regulation every fuckin' month. Just so they can shake down more money from Chinamen."

Preaching to the kitchen help, thought Jack.

"Ew ke ma ga hei, motherfucker," Billy cursed in his best Toishanese, the original tongue of the first immigrants to Chinatown. *"Thousands* of dollars in fines."

Jack picked up what he needed, went toward Billy who continued to vent in the general direction of the slop boys in the back. They frowned and nodded their heads at everything he said.

Feigning surprise, Billy turned to Jack and laughed, "Oh shit, it's Hawaii Five-0! Green cards out, everybody! *Book 'em,* Jack-O."

Jack was happy to see Billy grinning, a momentary departure from the edgy-depressive that Billy normally was.

"Wassup, man? You look like you got some *man tan* there." Billy took a breath, shook his head sadly as Jack plopped onto the counter the three plastic containers of *bok tong go* he'd taken from the refrigerator case.

"What's up with the crowd outside Sam Kee's?" Jack asked.

Billy chortled. "They're waiting for the free *for ngaap* duck. The inspectors said it's now illegal to hang ducks and chickens in the window, *without temperature controls.* Gave old man Kee a two-hundred-dollar fine, and a citation."

Jack was shaking his head, looking for *So what?*

"So the old man catches a fit, threatens to throw the ducks into the street. All the old folks are hoping to catch a freebie."

"It's not going to happen," Jack grimaced.

"I don't think so, either."

"All he'd be doing is inviting a Sanitation rap."

"Jack, yo, ducks and chickens been hanging in Chinatown windows a hundred years. All of a sudden it's a health issue?"

"Hundred Year's Duck. Isn't that the house special at Wally's?"

"It's all bullshit," Billy continued, "When was the last time we had an epidemic down here? Eighteen-ninety-three or something?"

Through the frosted street window Jack saw the green car with the sanitation sergeant seated inside, idling at the corner of Bayard.

"The city's just trying to pump bucks by pickpocketing the Chinamen, brother. Kee junior called it the Fuck the Duck Law. The Choke the Chicken Law."

Jack chuckled, knowing that the more things changed in Chinatown, the more they remained the same. *Been going on a hundred years.* Old Man Kee had probably been too slow with the payoff, or the department had sent an overzealous, perhaps racist inspector looking to advance. The Chinatown lawyers found ways to work around municipal regulations all the time. Administrations changed. This, too, would pass.

"Everybody's talking," Billy said quietly, "about the Ping woman. The Fukienese one who got killed?"

Jack nodded, the cause of the demonstration at One Police Plaza.

"Three hoodie-wearing punkass, hip-hop motherfucker wannabe thug gangsters." Billy's eyes steeled over. "And I lost

half the backroom boys yesterday 'cause they went to the protest at police headquarters."

"It ain't easy," Jack said.

"Fuckin' A that. The Fukienese Association wants the punks to
hang. They hired *white* lawyers even. Sorta like a *legal* lynching."

Jack checked his watch, thinking how long-winded Billy
could get.

"But crime never takes a holiday, huh," Billy joked. "So
what else you need, kid? Some *fun* or some *skin*?" Both were
references to tofu products, but sounded perverted with drug
and sexual innuendo.

The two of them broke out in laughter at this inside joke
that arose from the many sweaty hours they spent in the cook
room, boiling the beans.

Billy loosed a long sigh, adding, "You remember Jeff Lee?
Got a little office in a warehouse on Pike Street?"

"Sure," Jack said. "JK Trading, something like that."

"Well, he was asking for you. I tried calling you, then I
remembered you said you were away for vacation."

"Why? What's up?" Jack asked.

"Someone took like eight thousand worth of stuff, but they
didn't see no entry."

That's Ghost turf, thought Jack, *dailo Tat's territory.*

"No forced entry? Didn't Jeff call the cops?"

"Yeah, they came," Billy answered. "The burglary cops, you
know. They made a report, told Jeff they thought it was an
inside job." Billy leaned closer and said quietly, "Look, I told
Jeff you're out of the precinct, but he was just asking, maybe
you could take a look around. Like a second opinion."

Jack felt it again, the tension at the back of his neck, the reasons why he had to leave the Fifth Precinct. *The Chinatown way,* the Chinese mistrust of policemen and government officials, a historical divide covering centuries of corruption in China, and Hong Kong, where they'd refined corruption to an art form.

All the good things he accomplished as a cop here, made possible because he was Chinese.

All the bad things that happened along the way, also because he was Chinese.

Still, he thought he could have made a difference if only he could have kept his Chineseness out of it.

"C'mon," Billy snapped, breaking Jack's drift. "*What* fuckin' inside job? Jeff works the place with his father and sister. It's a desk and a coupla chairs, not JC Penney. They deliver to the vendors mostly. They don't get a lotta walk-in traffic out there."

"I had enough trouble in this precinct, Billy. I can't chump some other cop's report," said Jack.

"I'm not *saying* that, but if your own folks really *are* robbing you, you sure don't wanna hear it from some white cop who's laughing inside."

Jack shook his head at the raw truth in Billy's words.

"Don't worry about it, Jake. It's Chinatown."

"I'm *out,* Billy," Jack insisted.

"That's what I *told* Jeff," Billy half-protested. "Here, take his card anyway. Call him if you get any bright ideas."

Pocketing the card, Jack noticed the *United National,* a Chinese-language newspaper, on the counter. Plastered across the front page were photos of the Kung family murder-suicide. The headline TRAGEDY, reminded him to visit Ah Por, hoping for clarity. "You done with this?" he asked, folding up the newspaper.

"Take it," Billy answered.

"You heard about the shooting on Division? Players with AK-47s?"

"Yeah, it was on the radio," Billy remembered.

"What's up with that?"

"Don't know. I can check with the Fuk boys later. They're working the slop room in the afternoon."

"I'll call you tonight."

"It's Friday," Billy grinned. "You know where I'll be."

Jack smiled. Friday night was always right for Grampa's, a revered local bar dive.

The sky outside the Tofu King looked ominous again.

Billy put Jack's containers into a plastic bag, threw up his hands, palms out, and shook his head to refuse Jack's money.

Jack smiled and thumped his right fist over his heart to say thanks, and backed out through the cold, steamy door.

He took the shortcut down Park Street onto Mulberry, going along Columbus Park.

He didn't expect them to be there, the old ladies, but he wanted to be sure, and it was along the way. He was right. Not a soul here, the wind too cold, and the leaves long gone from the trees. In the warmer seasons, the old women lined the fence around the park, squatting low on plastic stools, with their charts, and herbs, and the red books containing their divinations. It was much too cold now, and Jack knew Ah Por would be indoors. He remembered her because Pa had gone to her those years after Ma died. Mostly it was for lucky words or numbers, or any kind of good news.

More recently, Ah Por's readings, in an oblique manner, had provided accurate clues for Jack. *The Senior Citizens Center,* he thought, stepping away from the park.

The dull red brick building hunkered down on the corner of Bayard under the flat sky, a stunted cousin to the art-deco colossus a block away at Baxter: the Tombs Criminal Facility, also known as the Men's House of Detention, and Criminal Courts Building. Its imposing facade was seventeen stories of cut limestone blocks, with solid granite at street level, circa 1938.

The red brick building was older, maybe a hundred years old. Its exterior was a blend of medieval-styled stonework, columns, and turrets. All the window frames were painted green. Jack remembered the place as his neighborhood grammar school, Public School 23, five stories of classrooms, auditorium, and cafeteria. Green linoleum throughout.

The school had served many generations of immigrants, including the Irish and the Italians. Ten years after Jack's all-Chinese class had graduated, the community outgrew the school, redirecting its sturdy rooms to servicing the senior citizens and the various cultural and civic organizations. They served free breakfast to seniors now, at the same lunch tables and benches that Jack remembered eating at as a schoolboy. Jack recalled those free lunches: cheese sandwiches, split-pea soup, macaroni-and-cheese, peanut-butter-and-jelly sandwiches. On rare occasions the kids would get a Dixie cup of ice cream.

When he stepped inside, it was as if the past had caught up with him, then surpassed him. The worn linoleum of his schooldays had been replaced by lighter vinyl tiles. Across the ceiling, hung new lighting, soft, but sufficiently bright for the elderly. The drone of people eating and talking filled the open space.

Chung Wah, Chinese radio, played news and weather over the PA system, just under the chatter and gossip.

Jack went toward the back of the room, where he saw that the old kitchen of the public school cafeteria had been refitted with a half-dozen gas-burning wok stations. Against the wall was a long shelf with five large commercial-grade electric rice cookers.

On a bulletin board, in Chinese characters, they'd posted the different menus for every day of the month. Soups: winter melon, lotus root, fish, or vegetables. Main plates: chicken wings, pork, salmon, or beef, pork chops, and Chinese sausage. Fruit of the day was usually oranges.

Jack looked out over the lunch tables, scanning the room for Ah Por, one old woman in a field of bundled gray heads, most of them wearing overstocked off-color down jackets, donated by Good Panda, the company logo prominently screened across their backs. He continued scanning, his eyes sweeping over more than a hundred Chinese seniors slurping their steaming breakfasts of boiled rice congee, *jook,* dipping the little bits of bread they'd brought along. A free bowl this morning, funded by some charitable organization, city agency, federal food program, or tong. *Whatever.* Jack was happy to see the elderly eating heartily, *jook,* the staple of their lives. Jack knew that Pa had come here for a few *jooks* in his day, if not for the sustenance, surely for the camaraderie.

Abruptly, he spotted her at the end of the bench by the far wall. The oversized down jacket made her appear smaller, huddled over her plastic bowl. When Jack came to her side the other seniors regarded him with curiosity and suspicion, but Ah Por didn't seem to notice him. *Probably her eyes are failing,* he thought, although he knew that the secrets she saw had nothing to do with her eyesight.

"Ah Por," Jack said, just loud enough above the din.

She looked up and after a moment, he saw small darts of recognition in her eyes. A thin, weary smile crossed her lips. He could see that she had none of her instruments of divination, no red booklet or cup of bamboo sticks, but he remembered she sometimes applied face reading to everyday items, and with a clairvoyant's touch, could provide a clue that, however obscure, proved to be on target.

This time, he needed consolation, clarity, more than a clue. Her words might exorcise the bad kharma clinging to him now.

"Ah Por," Jack repeated, handing her the *United National*, splayed open at the dead Kung family's photos. He pressed a folded five-dollar bill, folded square, into her ancient palm, gave her a smile, and a small bow of his head.

She ran a gnarled finger over the newsprint photos, closed her eyes. Slowly dropping her head to one side, as if straining to hear something, she said, "Fire." She paused, then softly, "It is a sign of sacrifice."

Her fingernails played over the text of the newspaper.

"Wind," she said, "blows away fear." Jack leaned in at the softness of her words.

"A *cleansing* is needed. Wash out the regrets. Sometimes it is necessary, to start anew." Her palm passed over the school-posed pictures of the children.

"There is no fault in this." Ah Por caught her breath, looked at Jack the way a grandmother looks at a schoolboy. "To be firm in punishment brings good in the end." She put out her hand and whispered, "Go to the temple, say a prayer, and make a donation. Eight dollars."

Jack palmed her another five-dollar bill, along with Jeff Lee's business card.

She rubbed up the card between her fingers, a look of annoyance crossing her face before she closed her eyes.

She said *"Malo."* Jack bent closer. *"Bad,"* she said. Bad, in Spanish? He was confused momentarily, until she opened her eyes, said it again. *"Ma lo,"* softening the Toishanese accent, meaning *monkey*.

"A monkey?" Jack asked. "You see a monkey?"

"A *picture*," Ah Por answered, suddenly flashing him a puzzled look. "You've been shot," she said matter-of-factly.

Jack was surprised that she knew. "Yes . . ." he started to answer, when she patted his left side under the jacket, where the ribs wrap around the heart.

"It was my arm," Jack continued.

"No," she said quietly. "Something else."

She's confused now, Jack thought. *Could be dementia there.*

"It was a while ago," he heard himself explaining.

"No," Ah Por repeated. "Not *when* . . ." Suddenly she started stirring the congee again, spooning up some, taking a slurp.

Jack knew the session was over. He thanked her, patted her gently across the shoulders. She seemed to shiver, and he backed away, leaving her to eat in peace.

She never looked up to see him leave the cafeteria of his childhood, more burdened now with answers he didn't understand.

Outside, he puzzled over Ah Por's words as he walked, the smell of Big Wang's *jook* and *yow jow gwai*, fried cruller, in the back of his mind.

Turning left on Bayard, he passed a string of tong basements that doubled as after-hours gambling dens. During the Uncle Four investigation, Jack's presence down in the dens had compromised several federal probes. His appearance had been duly recorded by DEA, and ATF, but he'd found out a female shooter could have been involved.

Someone, from one of the tongs, Jack figured, had also dropped a call to Internal Affairs, falsely accusing him of shaking down the gambling operators. The accusations had triggered an investigation, and he'd gotten suspended.

Somewhere, there was still a woman in the wind, he remembered, as he crossed Mott.

Pa's Jook

Big Wang, a longtime quick-food restaurant on Mott, still made congee the old Cantonese way, thick and clumpy, instead of more recent overseas styles that were watery, without substance. Jack remembered going to Big Wang's for Pa's favorite jook, ordering out a quart container each morning after Pa was no longer able to leave the apartment. Jack would deliver the *jook* to Pa before reporting to the Fifth Precinct, feeding his father each day of those last weeks of his life.

The congee, another reason why Pa had refused to leave

Chinatown. *His* jook, *his Chinese newspapers, his particular baby bok choy.* All his excuses to stay rooted.

When Jack's *jook* arrived, he dipped in a piece of *yow jow gwai,* fried cruller and let it soak up the congee, pondering Ah Por's words: *sacrifice, a monkey, and a gunshot wound.*

Hallucinations, mumbo jumbo, and witchcraft, Jack thought, but quickly remembered that her words had proven true in previous cases.

The congee had reminded Jack of Pa, and when he finished the bowl, he decided to visit the temple across the way.

Ma's Prayers

The gilded-wood carving above the Mott Street storefront read TEMPLE OF BUDDHA. In the window an elaborate wood carving featured the various monks and deities. A wooden statue of the Goddess of Mercy stood off to one side.

Inside, Jack heard Buddhist chanting from a tape in a boom box, saw red paper strips along the wall with black ink-brushed characters, the names of members and supporters. There was the smell of incense and of scented votive candles on pads floating in oil. In one corner, yellow plastic tags with the names of loved ones, the deceased arrayed in neat rows below the plates of oranges, the vases of gladiolas.

Imagining the death faces of the Kung family, he stepped up to the gods.

He lit three sticks of incense, bowed three times before the display of deities, and firmly planted the sticks in a sand-filled urn.

He thanked the sister monk, observing through the Buddha's picture window how busy the morning street had gotten.

On the way out he slipped eight dollars into the red donation box, and bid his farewell to the Kungs.

AJA

He walked briskly toward Chrystie Slip, where the street turned left and ran into NoHo. He exhaled puffs of steam as he went, saw that the cold prevented all but the hardy and unfortunate from walking the streets. Once past the junkie parks, he came to a storefront that was once a bodega, but now flew a big yellow banner that read ASIAN AMERICAN JUSTICE ADVOCACY.

The AJA, pronounced Asia, was a grassroots activist organization staffed by lawyers giving back to the community in pro bono time.

Inside the open storefront was a jumble of desks and office machines. There was no receptionist at reception out front, so he went directly toward Alex's little office in the corner.

He saw her through the small pane of glass in the wooden door. *Alexandra Lee-Chow, late twenties but could still pass for an undergrad, going through the beginning of a divorce, at the start of what was looking like a bad day.*

She was in a foul mood as he walked in. He hesitated. She waved him on, putting up a palm to silence him.

Jack put the plastic containers of *bok tong go* on the part of her desk that wasn't cluttered with files and legal documents.

He said quickly and quietly, "Just wanted to say thanks for Hawaii. And they told me you were out all morning."

Alex turned away, stating into the phone, "That's unacceptable. Shen Ping bled out waiting for the ambulance." She sat down, flashed Jack a disgusted look, and quietly hung up the phone.

"The Shen Ping killing." She rubbed her eyes. "You know, it's all over the news, with the protests and everything. Anyway, the family wants to sue the city, EMS, the criminal justice system." She paused. "And the NYPD, and anyone else connected to the killing."

Listening to her, Jack had already anticipated the complaint.

"EMS took more than twenty-five minutes to respond to the location," she began. "Out past Allen Street. The paramedics claim that commercial traffic, gridlock, boxed them in."

Jack listened patiently.

"Now, understand, local merchants have been complaining for months that *law enforcement—cops, court officers,* and other city personnel—abuse their parking permits by using Chinatown streets as their personal, long-term parking lot. DOT turns a blind eye to police parking but issues tickets to Chinese truckers who can't get to the curb and are forced to unload in the middle of the street."

Jack shook his head in sympathy.

She paused, only to say, "I'm sorry to blow this out on you, Jack."

"It's a rough day," he said. "I had a couple bad ones myself—"

"So my parents tossed you a *luau*?" Alex interjected, jerking the conversation another way.

Alex had hooked him up, he recalled, with the Hawaiian vacation package, when he'd needed the break badly, after his troubles in the Fifth. He'd been wounded, but still brought back a perp from San Francisco to cap the murder of Chinatown tong godfather Uncle Four. There had been a promotion at the end of it all.

"Yeah." Jack smiled, remembering. "Roast pig, poi, *mahi-mahi*, the works."

She nodded, smiled, then the hardness came back into her face.

"The kid who was the shooter," she said sourly, "had three outstanding warrants, and should have never been released from juvie. He had a history of violence and somebody screwed up."

The phone jangled again.

Jack could see it was important and started to leave.

I'll call you, he mimed with his index and pinky fingers, pausing at the door.

In turn, Alex pointed at the plastic containers. "Thanks for the *bok tong go*," she said quietly, smiling a sad smile as Jack backed away.

Day for Night

The sixteen-story mirrored glass office building at Two Mott Street was the tallest building in the area, anchored at street level by a Citibank branch and a tourist-trade gift shop. The On Yee Merchants Consortium was rumored to be one of the landlords, and they occupied the entire third floor, as well as the penthouse level. The tong made their *arrangements* in the penthouse, Lucky remembered, as he strode through the lobby.

It was the Ecstasy that was powering him through the nights, but now in the daylight, it kept him from the sleep he needed.

Lucky rode the closet-sized freight elevator to the roof landing and went to the far end. He took a deep gulp of the cold morning air, exhaled, and torched up a sensimilla joint, sucking deeply so that the tip burned a bright orange. The smoke settled him, allowed him to slow down, to see the bigger picture of the forces circling around him. When he looked out over the jumbled patchwork of rooftops, the expanse of Chinatown reached for the horizon. To the east, across the square, he saw the growing enclave of Fukienese Chinese immigrants, their Fuk Chow Native Association building flying the red flag of the People's Republic high above its tiled pagoda balcony.

Lucky remembered a childhood time when mainland supporters, the *commies*, would never dare fly the crimson flag for fear of being attacked and having their businesses vandalized or torched. Men wearing masks would come around, guns in their waistbands, to administer a beat down or a stabbing.

Times had changed.

While the old men of the tongs dithered with their deals, the young men who contested the streets had considerations of their own: controling the dirty money flowing through their rackets.

Lucky sucked heartily on the jay, scanning the view of old Chinatown, the core streets that the long ago Chinese bachelors first called home, eking out small lives under the heels of the whites, who didn't like them and didn't want them here. Still, the community grew. Now, the Fukienese were driving the boundaries north and east, their numbers swelling into the tenements that had housed the WASPs, the Irish, Italians, and Jews, and the Toishanese and Cantonese before them.

The windy rooftop refreshed him, and the marijuana brought him back down. His thoughts were still scattered from the Ecstasy, but he was beginning to see a pattern forming. As street boss of the Ghost Legion, Lucky was no student of history, but he was an admirer of the Romans, and before them, of the Mongolian hordes. He'd seen the videotapes *Rise and Fall of the Roman Empire,* with Chinese subtitles, and *The Great Khan,* both movies left behind by some loser in Number Seventeen gambling basement.

He'd learned that the Roman Empire collapsed because it became too large to manage, and corruption from within ate at it like a cancer. This is what he feared would happen to the Ghosts. Already his lieutenants in the Boston and Philadelphia Chinatowns were complaining that new bar clubs and card parlors had opened up, but away from the main streets. These new operators were members of village and fraternal organizations that were defiant when challenged. To help these upstarts, other groups like the Ma Ching—Malaysian gangsters—had arrived from the West Coast.

The New York Ghosts had gotten fat and comfortable, the complaint went, and they were reluctant to travel the interstate to muscle up their ranks. Lucky also knew that trouble was brewing in Chicago, with rumors that a splinter group of Ghosts was threatening to break away. More locally, the threat was Fukienese, challenging all comers to the long stretch of East Broadway and the side streets that ran like tentacles from it. Prostitution rackets from the snakehead sex slaves complemented gambling spots and the white powder of the China-based groups.

The more defiance there was at the fringes, the more *face* Lucky would lose and then more ambitious factions would question his leadership.

The Mongols were a different history. They conquered all, but were eventually swallowed up, becoming one with the peoples they'd overwhelmed. Like the Mongols, the big threat to Lucky lay to the East: China, Taiwan, and Southeast Asia. Would the old-line tongs, and the Hong Kong triads fall in step and sacrifice the Legion for more powerful paramilitary alliances from overseas?

Lucky sucked off the last of the joint, and flicked the burnt roach off the roof. He didn't like the thoughts of being sacrificed or swallowed up. *Trust no one* was the one motto he believed in. But like the Romans and the Mongols, wasn't it all *jing deng,* destiny? *If so, was there a way out for him? Take his fat accounts and run? Change his identity? Disappear?*

He laughed at his own momentary fear.

No need to panic, he thought. *There was plenty of time yet.* A pair of Chinese tour buses swung through Chatham Square below, bound for Atlantic City.

Lucky imagined cases of pills in the belly-holds of the coach buses stealing down I-95, a million tabs of Ecstasy rolling south from Montreal, party pills bound for clubs and dance joints all along the eastern seaboard. Tons of tax-free cigarettes from the Indian reservations. Let the Fuks ride shotgun on the deliveries. *Fuckin' A,* he thought, *the Ghosts could skip the muleing altogether, and just pick up the pills at the scheduled stops. They could spend more time on distribution. The volume would increase and the Legion would lessen its exposure and risk.* If the system worked well,

HENRY CHANG

Lucky could see alcohol, fireworks, AK-47s, and China White, all flowing down the pipeline.

Ka-ching ka-ching, already counting the money.

Lucky had heard other stories from the streets. Rumor had it, the Hung Huen—Red Circle Triad—had some unsatisfactory dealings with the Hip Chings.

Lucky considered his new grudging respect for the Hung Huen. *Green Circle, yellow circle, fuckin' pink circle, it was all the same to him; Chinese secret societies.* He saw it all as Fu Manchu bullshit that the whitey *gwailos* played, impressed by that crap with the candles and incense and chicken blood with the zombie chanting. In reality though, Lucky knew the triads were huge, sophisticated Chinese gangs that were major criminal players in Europe, and in Central and South America. More recently, they'd made inroads into North America by way of Canada.

Lucky knew he needed to be careful the Ghosts wouldn't be swallowed or sacrificed, yet he felt it was too early to set up a sit-down deal with the triads. See how the bus routes worked out first, Lucky figured. Besides, a partnership of the On Yee and the Bak Bamboo triad controlled the buses that carried junkets to casinos in Atlantic City and to Foxwoods in Connecticut. The Bak Bamboo was considering expansion of their routes to include Chinatowns within the tri-state area. He wanted to see what arrangements surfaced before he made his move.

See what happens, Lucky smirked, slowly remembering the value of patience in the face of change. He saw the red flag in the distance, and turned away from the cold wind that whipped in from East Broadway.

74

Sampan Sinking

Sai Go awoke on his sofa bed, still fully clothed except for his shoes, groggy and unsure how he'd gotten there. He had no idea what time it was, but in the somber light that crept in along the edges of the window blinds, he could make out the closet wall and the mirror above his dresser. Also, the two boxes of summer clothes he'd taken out in case he decided to go somewhere sunny and warm. It was early afternoon, but with a twilight sky outside his window. When he rolled out of the bed, he felt a twinge of pain in his shoulder and was reminded that he needed a haircut, which included a massage.

He pulled out a gray-metal lockbox from under the dresser, dialed the numbers until the combination was right, and opened it. There were the stacks of prepaid telephone calling cards, a few of which he used with his cell phones to take bets, a wireless transmission that couldn't be traced. Most of the cards were for sale, on consignment from Big Chuck Chan, who was the leading Chinatown distributor of international calling cards. All the gamblers knew Sai Go sold the cards and bought from him because of the dollar discount he offered. Big Chuck was one of Sai Go's regular bettors and the stack of phone cards served as collateral toward his credit line.

Underneath the stacks was a gun in a holster. He slipped the weapon out of the quick-draw belly-holster and caressed it. The Trident Vigilante was Italian-made, had a matte-nickel finish with black hard-rubber grips, and a six-shot cylinder that took the .32 caliber Smith & Wesson cartridge. The snub-nosed revolver was ultralight, only sixteen ounces, and the thirty-two cartridge produced less kick than the thirty-eight. It was a very practical belly gun, good for close combat but bad for distance accuracy. He had sawed and filed down the hammer so it wouldn't snag on the draw.

Sai Go didn't like automatic pistols because he worried they would jam up, and if he kept it on his belly with the safety off, he was afraid he would blow off his balls if he had to quick-draw and caught the trigger wrong. With the revolver, no such problems. Draw and shoot. No cocking action. Simple and quick. He'd seen enough gambler fights to know whoever got in the first hit was usually the winner. The first two shots, the muzzle explosions shocked the eardrums, causing a momentarily freeze. The man who didn't freeze up was going to walk away. The other man, dead.

Sai Go put his money on the revolver.

At the bottom of the box were two small packs of money, and an envelope that contained a booklet and a certificate for the fifty-thousand-dollar life insurance policy he'd bought from Nationwide. He had kept up the modest payments, all these twenty years since his wife left, thinking that if he ever remarried, he'd have something more to offer a woman than an aging divorced man who couldn't even claim a legitimate occupation.

The insurance was like a bonus prize, like a Ginsu knife.

He could remove his ex-wife's name as beneficiary and could designate a new beneficiary at any time. He didn't have children, had no one else in mind. Ha! The irony of it all, with him dying now, and no one else to benefit from it. The policy was paid up until next summer, a season he wasn't expecting to see.

He tucked the envelope back into the side of the box, and removed the packs of money, crisp twenties and fifties, a couple of thousand, emergency cash, run money. *Well, it was an emergency now,* he knew, and he with nowhere to run.

He imagined a village in the south of China, near Toishan, but far enough away from Guangjo city to still be considered farm country. The village of generations of his family, scattered now, the remaining few relatives there no longer on speaking terms with him, especially after the divorce. *Sure,* he thought, *go home to the village where no one wants me, so they can watch me die?*

He was calm, rested now after the long sleep. He had a vision of himself in Thailand somewhere, a sunny tropical vista with brown-skinned girls to ease his remaining days. Spend the nights drinking Singha beer and feasting on *satays, chow kueh teow* noodles, and *tom yum* soup.

When he thought better of it, he felt he could just as easily go to Fat Lily's or Angelina's for brown-skinned girls, and to Penang or Jaya Village for Thai beer, *roti,* and *hainam* chicken. For the sunny vista he could take a bus south on the interstate, or take the train with the glass skylight roof down to Florida somewhere for a few weeks. Somewhere sunny and not too far. A cruise to one of the islands? What would he do with a shipload of *lo fan* strangers? He could just as well be alone in Manhattan, if he only turned off his cell phones and stayed out of the OTB and Chinatown.

He was taking it all very well, he thought, with some resignation, of course, but what else could he do really? Get hysterical? Get depressed? Beg the gods for forgiveness and salvation? Be hopeful even when the doctors offered no hope? He wasn't the suicidal type, and even though he feared the pain to come, he didn't see himself wasting half the time he had left being sick from the radiation. He wasn't going to roll up in bed and wait to die.

He'd made it to fifty-nine, Sai Go mused, *what the hell.* He'd led a decent life, generally speaking, and hadn't committed any evil he couldn't face up to.

There were no relatives to notify. He wasn't leaving anything to anyone, and his plot in the old Chinese section of Peaceful Valley cemetery had been paid in full years ago. Now he needed to spend whatever he had left, and try to avoid a painful death, even though he'd quit the meds, and canceled the chemotherapy.

Three or four months?

If he were a family man, there would be many other considerations, but he was alone. So the question was did he really want to go on a vacation to die, or to hang around Chinatown until the end? He could stop taking bets and just enjoy the final days. Take a junket to Atlantic City or Connecticut and play some cards games with the Chinese high rollers. He'd get comped with a lot more bang for the buck, and it would be only a three-hour bus ride from Chinatown.

The thoughts went back and forth inside Sai Go's head even as he slurped hot *jook*, and chewed the crisp fried crullers at Big Wang's. He read his Chinese newspapers and couldn't help but scan the racing sections.

At the U.S. Asia Bank, his Happy Valley payout had been wired, and now his account had grown to over thirty-eight thousand. Even minus the six thousand for the *dailo*, he still had over thirty thousand to spend during his last months. There was another two thousand on the street he had to collect, but he didn't anticipate a problem. These bettors were his family: the waiters, cooks, kitchen help, the street vendors and deliverymen. Ten-dollar bettors and hundred-dollar players, he'd treated them all fairly, with a savvy blend of camaraderie and no-nonsense. He never let his credit get too far in front and had built a loyal following. None of which mattered anymore, Sai Go knew, the game was over.

He went east on Catharine Street toward Henry, those streets crowded even in the cold with sidewalk vendors of fruit, vegetables, and seafood stores stacked against meat and poultry markets and a string of bakeries. Trucks and vans idled at the curb, their exhaust pipes steaming, as they rushed their deliveries with one eye out for the *chow pai* ticket of the *brownie* traffic cops.

On Henry Street, the buildings were turn-of-the-century brick tenements, mostly Jewish back then, but now overwhelmingly Chinese. A section of the Manhattan Bridge rose up in the near distance.

The New Canton Hair Salon had a blue awning with a cartoon of a pair of scissors and a comb drawn across the front. It was a small storefront sandwiched between a noodle shop and a poultry market on a dilapidated block of Henry Street.

The salon was unlike the new and shiny hair, nail, and massage "emporiums" that dominated Pell and Doyers Streets. There was graffiti on the outside of the New Canton. Inside was a run-down room with six barber chairs and a small counter near the door. There were mirrors on the walls, and shelves full of shampoo, lotions, and towels. The helpers washed hair at two basin stations, side by side behind a plastic partition.

As he approached, Sai Go could see there were two barbers on duty and no customers in the shop. One cutter was a vampy-looking Chinese girl with reddish hair, who showed a lot of skin and a tattoo of a cat on her shoulder. The other was Sai Go's regular, a woman he knew as Bo, which meant precious. She'd been trimming his hair once a week for almost two years now.

Ms. Chu Bo Jan.

Bo was not one of the full-time stylists, the pro hair designers. Instead, she rented one of the barber chairs three to four days a week for a sixty-forty split between her and the salon owner. The owner, KeeKee, was an occasional bettor with Sai Go, and she had explained Bo's situation when he inquired, privately, why an older woman, still handsome, had come to be a part-time haircutter.

Precious

Bo was indebted to the snakeheads, one of many thousands who were paying off a thirty-thousand-dollar deal with Chinese human traffickers, for passage to America. The deal involved bogus passports, fraudulent paperwork, and sometimes the promise of jobs. The illegals placed relatives in China as human collateral against breaking the contract.

Bo Jan was twenty-eight, already considered an old lady, when she'd married a factory worker ten years older than herself. This was during the times of the One Child Policy. Bo had wanted a child, and her husband Kwok grudgingly agreed that a child would be okay if it were a boy. The option of an abortion was already in the back of his mind.

It was a girl.

The marriage quickly became strained. Kwok wanted to give up the baby girl to an orphanage, as many Chinese had done. He hoped they'd have another chance at a coveted boy child.

Bo could not bear the thought.

The orphanages were flooded with baby girls. Americans, who'd declined to adopt black American babies, were flocking to China to adopt yellow babies as fast as they became available. China was selling its unwanted excess population at ten thousand dollars an adoption. This new global baby trade was sanitized, and legal. The Asian women sex-slaves who arrived packed in the holds of cargo ships had no such protection.

Rather than allowing the clan bloodline to end, Kwok abandoned his wife and child before the baby girl was a year old. Bo took her daughter back to her family village near the Pearl River. There, a series of unsuccessful relationships with local village men caused her to lose hope of a future for her in China, where she would be doomed to wind up a spinster, with a mother and a young daughter to care for. She began to hope for a new start in America. After the girl's third birthday Bo left, alone, smuggled by snakeheads to New York City by way of Canada.

Now, after two years of slaving in Chinatown, she was still struggling to pay off her passage, the specter of prostitution ever present.

At first the snakeheads tried to convince her to become a whore, to work for an escort service, saying it was a much faster way to repay the debt, adding that she was not such a young woman anymore.

She had politely declined their offers and never bowed to their intimidation. Bo explained to these heartless men with no souls that she was a devout Buddhist, and prostitution was a grave sin. The snakeheads ridiculed her, called her crazy, *chi seen,* but by slogging through a succession of small jobs, she managed to pay her monthly installment to them without fail. She worked in a Chinatown bakery during the day, supplementing her salary with piecework, *cheun gee,* at home, where she strung beads into necklaces, or assembled gift baskets. The payments to the snakeheads continued, as did the funds she wired to her mother and daughter in Toishan.

After a year, the bakery job became a supermarket cashier post, which became a gift-shop clerkship, the jobs declining in desirability, requiring longer hours for less pay. So, in rapid succession, she snipped threads off piecework in a sweatshop, pushed a steamy dim sum cart in a restaurant, gutted tilapia in a fish market. On Canal Street, she hawked knock-off designer handbags. In between, she washed hair and swept up the shorn locks that piled up beneath the rotating chairs in the barber shops that lined Doyers Street. She taught herself how to cut men's hair, and learned to include a free ten-minute neck and shoulder massage.

She waited until Sai Go was seated comfortably in the chair before she draped the plastic sheet over him.

He observed his haggard reflection in the mirror, noticed when she glanced at him. She held her small smile.

"I didn't see you last Saturday, you weren't here," she said matter-of-factly.

"Of course not." He smiled quietly. "How could you see me if I wasn't here?"

"I thought you found a new cutter," she teased. "At one of the *designer* shops, hah?"

Sai Go grinned. She was happy to see this as her comb and electric clipper danced, spraying bits of gray and white hair off his head, small clumps catching on the plastic sheet around him.

"One of those young girls made up like Hong Kong movie stars?" Bo continued, "A *siu jeer* girl to cut you a new style, hah? Give you a great massage, make you feel like young man again, hah?"

Sai Go chuckled, told her again and again that it was just some family business that had come up. He remembered she had given him the gold-plated Buddhist card, the talisman, many haircuts ago. He'd explained to her then that in his line of work he dealt with good people and bad people alike, explaining why he carried a box cutter in his back pocket.

Bo had detected sadness in him then, and still now, in this older man who she guessed was about twenty-five years her senior. She felt sorry for him, and tried to cheer him up with clever sayings, giving him five extra minutes of shoulder massage. The Buddhist talisman had been one of several that she carried to ward off the sex-slave snakeheads. She'd told him it would protect him in his travels.

Sai Go's haircut hadn't required much imagination. Years of ministrations by Chin Ho's barber shop on Doyers Street had shaped his hair into a military-style crewcut, the sides trimmed very tight to the skull, the top about an inch long and angled back. Bo rubbed gel into the top so the sheen would disguise the gray there. He looked younger than a man in his fifties, she thought, although this day he looked tired, a bit distant, his mind drifting elsewhere.

When he looked in the mirror, Sai Go saw a beat-up, baggy-eyed fifty-nine-year-old mask of wrinkles, worry lines etched into his brow. Fifty-nine—the numbers five and nine, in Chinese sounded like *not enough. True,* he thought, *Not enough luck, not enough time . . ."*

"It's the massage," he heard Bo say, still teasing. "Must be I give a better massage, hah?"

Sai Go smirked, closing his eyes as the roar of the blow-dry gun filled his ears.

Bo released the lever and the chair dropped so that she had a higher angle to work from.

It *was* the massage, he thought, the only time he'd ever felt tension leaving his body. He liked the way Bo dug her elbows into the tops of his shoulders. He shut his eyes as she pressed down harder into the deep part of the muscle, then dragged her elbows along his shoulder blades. Her fingers worked the joints, pressing nerve points that ran along the spine.

Bo had strong fingers and hands, and knew just how much force Sai Go could tolerate.

"Everything's stiff," she said innocently. "*Very hard.* What have you been doing? See? Miss a week and your back's all screwed up."

"You're right," he heard himself say. "I'll try not to miss any more visits."

She said, "You're working too hard, that's what it is. You need to drink hot soup. Wintermelon, *foo jook,* mushrooms." She gave him a pat on the back. "It's the wintertime. You know how to make soup, don't you?"

She put her thumbs into the depressions at the base of his skull and worked the nerves, then followed with hands, firmly grabbing, kneading the musculature and cords inside the back of his neck.

He took a long and deep breath, held it a moment before releasing it, thinking, *He was fifty-nine, and she was thirty-something, yet she was mothering him?*

Bo's pressing and digging, pushing and rubbing, forced his inner energy, his *chi*, to circulate. He felt his blood moving, the joints of his fingers crackling as he clenched and unclenched his fists underneath the plastic sheet. Finally, she balled her fists and pounded his back. *Playing the drum*, it was called.

When she was done, he gave her his usual ten-dollar tip, generous but not so overly generous that it suggested anything more than simple appreciation of services received. Knowing her story, Sai Go felt sorry for her, for her predicament, supporting two generations back in China, and having to fend off the snakeheads.

After Sai Go left the New Canton, Bo had begun to sweep up the hair on the floor around her station when she noticed the folded square of paper directly underneath the chair. It was a prescription card with notations she didn't understand, from the Mon Tang Pharmacy on Mott Street. Folded along with the card was a piece of notepaper from Chinatown Imaging, and a scrap of crinkly cellophane that had the Chinese words *Ming Sing*, or movie star, scrawled on it.

On the Chinatown Imaging note was the word chemotherapy with appointment dates during previous weeks. They all seemed to be Thursdays. Below the dates was a scribble of Chinese words, several of which she understood to mean *cancer* and *radiation*.

A freezing wind suddenly swept into the salon, and Bo quickly glanced toward the door, but she knew that Sai Go was long gone. She stepped out into the cold street anyway, looking both ways to make sure he wasn't still in sight.

Back inside the shop, Bo tucked the papers into her pocket, and reminded herself to return them on his next visit. She realized then why Sai Go had missed his last trim and although she hadn't noticed any hair loss, he did appear fatigued, quieter than usual. The word *radiation* lingered in her mind, and she considered whether there was another talisman that could prevent the pain of cancer.

Friends

At eleven, the Sunset Park waterfront shimmered in the frosty moonlight far below his studio window. Dressed for the chill, Jack was adjusting the holster with the Detective Special on his hip when his cell phone trilled. Seeing Alexandra's name appear in the little window above the keypad, he was surprised, because the only times she'd ever called before was when he was on the job.

"Hey, what's up?" he asked.

"Did I catch you at a bad time?" Alex sounded tired.

"No, I was just going to drop by Grampa's."

There was a short pause, as if she were sipping a drink or something. "Right. Got a question about a permit for a gun," she said.

"*Shoot.*" He felt himself grinning.

"The application process is real complicated, I hear."

"Wait, who's this for?"

"Myself."

"You?"

"Long story."

"Well," he checked the Timex on his wrist, "give me the short version."

"There was a smuggled girl we put up in the shelter. In the last few days, Doris has been getting nasty threatening calls at the reception desk."

"What kind of threats?"

"'Stay away from our women.' 'Your office may catch fire.' Crap like that."

"No shit. In Chinese?"

"Mandarin, sort of."

"Sort of?"

"Doris said, with a sort of accent, like Fukienese, maybe. Two nights ago, when we closed, two guys were peering in through the blinds. After that, I felt like someone was following me, like from a distance."

He pulled his black North Face jacket from the little closet.

"Fukienese?" he asked.

"Chinese, for sure. Last night I thought I saw one of them outside Confucius."

"Go to the precinct and file a Form Sixty-One report so it'll be on record. And it could support your pistol application." He paused, checking for his keys. "You still have that friend in the DA's office?"

"Yes," she said.

"Well, you're a lawyer yourself. That will help. But the DA's office could call the Licensing Division. Know what I'm saying?"

"Right."

"After you get the paperwork in, I'll set you up at a pistol range. Learn how to shoot the right way. I know a guy on the West Side. Nice guy, *Chinese,* too."

"Yeah, sure." He heard her chuckle. "Thanks a lot." It sounded like she took another sip, before saying, "There's some other stuff . . ."

He checked his watch again.

"Tell you what," he said. " Why don't you drop by Grampa's later?"

He thought he heard *"You bet"* before she hung up.

Golden Star

The Golden Star Bar and Grill on East Broadway was known to the locals as Grampa's, a revered Chinatown jukebox joint frequented by a Lower East Side clientele of Chinese, Puerto Ricans, blacks, and whites. It was three steps down to a big room with an oval-shaped bar, and even in the dim blue neon light, Jack could make out Billy seated at the end of the long glossy counter. He was watching two Latinas shooting a rack on the pool table in the back.

Jack took a barstool next to him.

"Hey hey," greeted Billy. "Wassup?"

"You tell me," answered Jack. "What's the buzz?"

"Just a coupla the Fuk slop boys talking," Billy said, signaling the bartender for a beer for Jack. As he waited, Jack remembered Vincent Chin, editor of the Chinese language newspaper, the *United National.* He had assisted Jack in the past. Jack knew Billy's words would be neighborhood lowdown, in contrast to Vincent's professional view.

They tapped beer bottles and Billy swiveled on the barstool, put his back to the two ladies at the pool table and leaned toward Jack. "In the slop room," he said quietly, "I overheard the Fuk boys talking about the big shootout under the bridge. The crap didn't start there, and probably won't be the end of it. A coupla weeks ago, some Fuk Ching gangbangers threw a beat down on a few casino bus drivers who weren't knuckling under. What happened the other night, the young guns chased a Fuk Chow crew chief down Henry, through the backstreets near the bridge. They shot him as he ran. Six times, both legs and arms."

"They let him live," Jack said, knowing now why the shooting never made the blotter as a homicide.

"It was a warning." Billy continued, "The young Chings felt they were being squeezed out of the tour-bus game, like a new deal was coming down. The older Fuk Chow guys didn't like the attention the young guns were attracting."

"Well, too late now." Jack smirked. "The shit's hit the fan. Whatever the shady bus deal was, there's a spotlight on it now, and they can't be happy about that."

"That's a bet," said Billy. "And about Jeff's office getting robbed out there? The slop boyz claim that the Ching crews ain't into burglaries. They don't want stuff they gotta resell. They only want *cash* money, gold and silver. Easy money, jacking home invasions, kidnap, strong-arm. They threaten the victims to keep them quiet. The victims don't really want to pull in the cops, get deported. It's a win-win deal for the bad boyz."

Jack remembered Ah Por's bad, monkey vision, and kept silent. He knew that a third of cases went unresolved, and if

Jeff's family members were really robbing him, would he want it made public? To bring the family shame?

Cold Case came to his mind.

"Guess it's just another mystery," Billy said, turning his attention back to the Latinas, one of whom sank the eight ball, and was squealing gleefully, her breasts jiggling.

"Rack," she said to the other woman.

"*Rack* is right," agreed Billy, admiring her cleavage, and earning a smile from her.

Jack saw Alexandra come through the front door and slide into one of the booths. He patted Billy on his shoulder. "Catch you later," Jack said, gliding off the barstool. He left Billy at the bar watching the Dominican ladies work a new rack, two beers still on ice. For him, the night was still young and full of possibilities.

He slipped into the booth next to Alex, ordering another beer as the waitress brought her a cloudy martini. Alex torched up a cigarette, took a French diva's drag.

"Go for broke?" Jack teased. "Every man for himself?"

"Sure, no prisoners tonight." She grinned.

"When did you start drinking those?" Jack asked. He remembered the morning she'd been escorted into the Fifth Precinct by one of the female uniforms, holding back on a D&D only because Alexandra had dropped his name. The *drunk and disorderly* had turned out more disorderly than drunk, with Alex still fuming after she'd tossed her cheating ex-husband's Italian suits out of their eighteenth-floor condo at Confucius Towers.

The husband was angry, but not about to press charges.

Jack had gotten it straight with the woman cop, thanked her for backing off the D&D, for giving him face, cop to cop.

He'd given Alex a stern talking to about the evils of alcohol, before releasing her.

Alex blew out a stream of smoke through the o of her lips, smiling. "You think work's driving me to drink?"

"I think it's driving you nuts." He smiled, reluctant to judge her when his own fist was wrapped around a drink.

"How's the little girl?" Jack asked, strangely feeling a sense of duty.

"Chloe's with her father this weekend," she said with a frown. They were quiet a moment, looking to lose the subject. They clinked glasses.

Alex sipped, watching Jack draw back a big gulp.

"After you left the other day," she said, "a girl came in. She was about nineteen. The snakeheads brought her over and she was paying off the passage. The owner of her sweatshop absconded with the money, the place closed, and she was out of work. Couldn't make the payments." Alex worked the martini down. "They tried to make a whore out of her," she said quietly. "She refused and got a beating. Now we have her in our women's shelter. She's afraid they'll find her, and she's desperate for a job."

Jack put a gentle hand on Alex's shoulder. "You can't save *everyone*, Alex."

" For the ones that fall in my lap, I know I can make a difference."

"And I *know* you will." They touched glasses again.

"To the *struggle*," she said, irony in her voice. She sounded bitter, and after a slow, lingering sip, she said, "So here's my question. What can be done, in terms of law enforcement, to stop these snakeheads?"

Jack narrowed his eyes. "Hasn't she gone to the precinct?"

"She's too afraid."

"Get an Order of Protection."

"That's a joke." She exhaled a menthol puff sideways.

"Set up a sting? Agree to pay up and catch them when they show up to collect."

"Come on, Jack. She's even more afraid of that."

"Then get her to relocate. Start over somewhere else, preferably far away. You can't always deal with the snakeheads using courts and cops."

"How then?"

"It's an underworld thing. You get a rival group to go against them."

"What happens?"

"Whatever it is, gets settled. Money. Face. Whatever."

"So the scum take care of their own?"

"Something like that."

He watched her work the drink down, a frown returning to her lips.

"Look, just call the precinct," Jack advised. "If you see anything funny, like men loitering on the block, maybe they'll roll a car by."

"We filed three police brutality cases with the Civilian Complaint Review Board last year. You think that'll happen?"

"And if you got pepper spray, anything like that, don't be afraid to use it."

"Jack?"

"Yeah?"

"You don't think I'm just being paranoid, do you?"

"No, but *are* you?"

She drained the glass, signaled the waitress for a refill.

"We take on difficult cases," she said distantly. "It's not like we haven't received threats before."

"So what's different *here?*"

"I don't know. It feels a little more *personal.* I don't know. I just don't know."

"Well, you have to be careful. Be alert, know who's around you. It's still New York City, *lady.*"

Jack remembered that she was already under stress from her legal work on the Ninety-Nine Cents shooting incident.

"What's gonna happen with the Ping woman's lawsuits?" he asked.

"They're going to work their way through the courts. There's a lot involved. It'll be a long time before anyone sees justice," she replied. Her second drink arrived and she took a quick sip, keeping the glass at her fingertips. "How about you?" she asked, leveling a look at him. "You look tanned, but tired."

"Yeah, soon as I got back from Hawaii I caught a murder-suicide. The whole family, gone."

"Was this the Taiwanese family?"

Jack nodded, taking a gulp from the bottle.

"It's in the papers everywhere." She shook her head. "How sad. You caught that case, huh?"

Jack nodded stoically, drained his bottle, and ordered a whiskey shot.

After two martinis, Alex slowly became unfocused, making a kamikaze dive into the no-pain zone. Jack downed the whiskey shot. He knew she'd needed to vent and he was glad he'd been available. He glanced at his watch, gave a credit card to the waitress, and put his arm across Alex's shoulders.

"Thanks again for Hawaii," he said.

"Least could I do," she slurred.

Jack grinned. "Time to go, lady."

The dark streets ran down toward Confucius Towers. Jack considered walking Alex directly to her apartment door, weighing it against the implication of escorting a tipsy, high-strung, and vulnerable woman going through a divorce, who was coming home to an empty apartment for the holidays.

The term she'd used, *irreconcilable differences,* came to his mind.

He was still considering as they reached the main gates of the Towers.

"Thanks," Alex said firmly, pushing Jack away gently with her palms. "I'm okay from here."

"Sure . . . ?" Jack asked. It appeared the night air had revived her.

"Sure. And thanks a lot."

"For what?" Jack smiled.

"For listening." She smiled back. "See ya," she called as she marched toward the high-rise, swaying slightly as she went.

Jack watched until she was inside the guarded lobby, inside the elevator.

Turning away from the Bowery, Jack took a deep swallow of icy air and stepped off the curb between parked cars, looking for a taxi back to Brooklyn. He didn't see any cabs at the corner. The light turned red.

Behind him, a dark form rolled up, and he recognized the low rumble of the engine even before he saw the black Riviera, running without headlights, boxing him in between the cars. Instinctively, he brushed his gun hand against the grip of the Colt.

He was not surprised when Tat Louie, one-time blood brother and now Ghost Legion *dailo,* came out of the back of the car.

"Hey, homeboy." Lucky grinned. "I mean *officer.* Oh, I mean *detective.*"

"Keep it up, Tat," Jack answered evenly. "If this car don't move *now,* I got cause to look inside. Wanna bet I find a piece in there?" Now he grinned back. "Maybe on your big, ugly gorilla boy?" He shaped his hand like a gun, tapped the barrel finger against the tinted passenger window, imagining Kongo there.

Lucky's smile turned into a sneer. He nodded at the driver's window, and Lefty slid the Buick forward a body's length. Lucky stepped up to Jack and they faced off between the parked cars.

Jack fired first. "What do you want, Tat?" He remembered that Internal Affairs had accused him of *associating with known felons,* of the *extortion of Chinatown businessmen.*

"You got news and I'm buying. Let's talk, *brother man.*" Lucky lit up a smoke.

"We *had* that converation already," said Jack, no patience on his face.

"Bullshit. You weren't *listening* the last time. You didn't wanna hear it. Just kept talking all that *give up* stuff. Your blue boyz took down Number Seventeen, and Fat Lily's. But you know that. So what's up, *brother?* Why are they targeting us? And then I find out you left the precinct. I thought you liked it here. Fight crime, all that."

"Fuck you, Tat."

"Aw, come on now. You know what? I think, inside, you like it here. You'll be back. You're the Chinese cop, remember? The new sheriff in town, gonna turn everything around. Ha, you think you make a difference? It's *Chinatown,* man. Come on, give me a heads-up. I'll help you make captain."

"I don't need the headache."

"Right. You'd rather roll around in the gutter. You like to hang with those *gwailo* micks and guineas, with their stupid Chinaman jokes?"

"Kiss my ass."

"Break it out then. You going *gay-lo* on me?" He smiled, softening his approach. "Look, what's it take? I know, I know, money and pussy don't interest you. You don't like the bling-bling, the nice threads, the sexy cars?"

"You got nothing I want. If I needed all that, I'd get it on my own."

"What the fuck? You think you're gonna do twenty and get out? Then be a security guard somewhere?" Lucky hissed. "All I want is information. I ain't asking you to get your hands dirty. Shit, you mean to tell me you'd rather side with the *gwailos,* man? You choose them fuckin' mooks who used to laugh at us and call us *chingchong wingwong*? Boy, you ain't nothing but a Charlie Chan, hah."

Jack didn't take the bait, tossed it back at Lucky. "Here's one for you, big boss. *Lucky* man. Your boys supposedly run the streets out here, right? Remember the warehouses down on Pike? The ones we used to run through? Well, someone's busting rip-offs there. That used to be your turf, right?"

"Still is," Lucky spat out, taking the bait.

"So that means . . . it's *your* boys pulling the jobs?"

"Didn't say that. And don't try to punk me, kid. You ain't made for it."

"Maybe it's not really your turf. Lots of Fuks and Dragons out here. Maybe they're eating your *dim sum* again."

"Ha ha, funny. You got jokes, son. But what's it to you? You a partner?"

"Friend of mine got robbed. Any ideas?"

Lucky smiled, feeling the leverage shifting. "Not right now, Jacky boy. But let's say I get a tip on a raid, or maybe, a surveillance setup. Or give me a heads-up, *Whatcha gonna do when they come for you, bad boy?* Maybe then something might occur to me, *capisce?*" He chuckled at the wop word, backstepping to the black car. Before sliding inside, he said, "Give me a sign, Jacky boy. *Give me a sign.*"

"Get out while you can. It's the last time I say it, *Nothing I can do when they come for you . . .*"

Jack could hear hyena laughter from inside the car as it growled and sped off, leaving a cold trail of vapor and smoke.

After a minute the night streets went quiet, and when the traffic light turned green again, Jack caught a yellow cab that took him back across the bridge.

Dailo's Money

Sai Go stood inside the front vestibule of the OTB, just beyond the cutting wind that sliced inside each time anyone went in or out.

He kept a watchful eye on the streets that crossed Chatham Square, looking for the black car coming for the *dailo*'s cash in his pocket.

It was 1 AM in the dead of night.

In his mind he saw palm trees and Mickey Mouse, and a pack of gray dogs wearing numbers, yelping as they dashed around an oval track.

The Gold Carriage Bakery was promoting a Holiday Special to Disney World in Orlando, and Longshot Lee had signed on for the vacation junket along with two of the *da jop*, kitchen help. Chat Choy had called Sai Go and asked him to come along, saying Gum Sook also had committed to the trip and had brewed up a thermos full of special herbal tea for him.

They could all bet on the dogs together.

So he agreed, and they were off the next day. Meet early, get a few *baos*, and tea, before getting on the bus. Bring a few newspapers. He could sleep along the way if he felt tired.

The Special included a floor show with Hong Kong singers and dancers, and a Chinese lunch buffet the entire week.

The dingy fluorescent light that spilled out of the OTB cast morbid shadows all around as the black car rolled to a smooth stop at the curb. Behind the dark windows, Lucky recognized Sai Go pacing around inside the vestibule, as he'd been instructed to do.

Lefty flashed the headlights twice, keeping the horn silent.

They watched Sai Go come out of the OTB, then Lefty killed the lights. Sai Go stepped carefully along the frozen street, looking the car over as he went. The back window powered down, and he saw the *dailo*'s eyes.

"Get in," said Lucky.

There was plenty of room for Sai Go as he slid onto the cushioned backseat. He handed over an envelope, saying, "Six thousand eight hundred."

"And I know I don't have to count this, right?" Lucky glanced at him sideways.

"Only if you like," Sai Go said quietly.

Lucky counted a thousand out of the envelope and slipped the bills onto the backseat next to Sai Go.

"That's yours," Lucky said. "For Koo Jai. The matter is closed."

"Thank you, *dailo*."

"We don't need to speak of it again."

"Understood." Sai Go exited the car, saying "Thank you" again as the Riviera pulled away to make the green light. Standing by the curb in the wind, his frosty breath curling out, he pressed the extra thousand in his pocket, squeezed the wad into a roll.

The black car skirted a turn around the Square and headed uptown.

Sai Go turned and walked away from the OTB, thinking about the odds at the dog tracks, and the warm Florida sun. The group had planned an early start, and he was already feeling tired, hunched up against the gusts that grabbed at each trudging step home.

From the rearview mirror, Lucky saw Sai Go move off the Square, and turned his thoughts to Koo Jai, the *wiseass*, but he decided to keep to himself the knowledge of paying the little brother's debt. For now anyway. Lucky realized the possibility that Koo Jai was the real culprit behind the rip-offs, but Skinny Chin had gone to Hong Kong and wasn't due back until after Christmas. *Kid Koo ain't going nowhere,* figured Lucky. *It'd keep until Skinny got back.*

Lefty urged the car back toward Mott, checking his watch, and marking the time.

Hovel and Home

The building at 98 East Broadway was a dilapidated four-story red-brick tenement near Mechanics Alley, beneath the roar-and-rumble racket of the subway trains, trucks, and mini-buses banging across the Manhattan Bridge. The building had a Chinese convenience store in a step-down basement and a cosmetics chain store six steps up the side stairs. On the sidewalk an old Chinese woman, wrapped in a shabby down coat, sat behind a folding table that dangled socks and thermal underwear, plastic sandals, ball caps, and batteries.

The back of Number 98 had a fire escape leading from the fourth floor down to a sliding metal ladder that dropped into a tiny yard closed off by an eight-foot-high fence. On the other side of the fence was a parking lot and a small shed where the broccoli vendor stashed his hundred daily cases.

The old apartments were railroad flats, long and narrow, running from the front to the back of the building, two apartments per floor. What had once been a communal bathroom in the hallway had been converted to two closet-size bathrooms, one for each apartment. Each had a tiny window that vented out back, to the parking lot.

In tenement flat number two, Koo Jai stood by the window, naked in the dim daylight, looking through the window blinds to the icy streets below. The afternoon was overcast and static with mist that promised to turn to snow.

On East Broadway and Market, four Fukienese youths stood together, one with gel-spiked hair flanked by two others in black leather jackets, their hands tucked into their pockets against the cold. Koo Jai couldn't see their eyes behind their flashy black sunglasses, but he felt they were up to no good. The fourth youth stood to one side, a rangy, solid-looking kid who kept his right hand inside the slash pocket of his black trench coat. He was slowly rocking from side to side, in a *tai chi* kind of way, his eyes peering over the edge of sunglasses, sucking in every movement in the intersection.

Fucking Fuks, thought Koo Jai. The cold of the front room felt good against his overheated skin. He remembered why he'd left the thick heat of the back room, and reached down beneath the window. He pulled up a short piece of baseboard, extracted a plastic-wrapped bundle, then slipped the board back in place.

When he peered through the blinds again, the four Fuks were gone and he wondered which of the Chinatown shopping malls they were going to hang out in.

Up to no fuckin' good, he knew.

For a moment, he scanned the small dark room. There was the bulk of the faded black leather couch, a convertible number that had to be ten years old, one of the surviving pieces of furniture from when the apartment had been the Stars' clubhouse, where the gang partied and brought their girl-friends for sex. This was when their brotherhood controlled these streets, before their leader Tiki, and three senior brothers, mysteriously disappeared, before the Ghosts rolled in with a hundred men and took over.

There was a cheap folding table in one corner and an array of mismatched shelf units and clothes cabinets stretching the length of the long wall leading to the back bedroom. Three metal chairs were folded, leaning against the table, in case he had visitors.

For a long time now, except for Shorty coming by occasionally to smoke a joint and down a beer, he never had *visitors*, and the place had become his apartment, drug den, love nest, whatever. The Jung brothers, Old Jung and Young Jung, were too lazy to climb even the one flight of stairs, and since he didn't have a television set, they were even less inclined to drop by and hang out. *Just as well*, he thought, no interruptions when he brought his girls up, and less chance of any of the gang stumbling upon his stash of the loot they divvied up. He used the spot behind the baseboard at the window. Another spot was under the floorboards, beneath one of the full-length wall mirrors he'd got from Job Lot, the other one mounted in the back room, strategically placed so that he could see himself with the parade of women he brought to his bed.

He unwrapped the plastic bundle and admired the dozen watches inside. Six Rados, four Cartiers, and two Rolexes. Twenty-five gees worth of fine timepieces and he'd taken the best for himself. Shorty'd gotten a Rolex and a half dozen Movados, as had each of the Jung brothers. He removed one of the Rados, a gold woman's piece that had a modern metallic bracelet and a square black face with diamond baguettes arranged on all four sides.

He held one of the Rolexes, ran his thumb along the watchband, across the face, caressing, *feeling* its mechanical splendor. He heard again the words of the *dailo* still ringing in his ears: *If there's another rip-off, it's gonna be on you.*

Warnings from the *dailo*, whom he never saw except when he came to collect cash or to complain, this end of East Broadway being too far from the lucrative streets around Mott and Bayard, Canal and Pell, for social visits, were not too impressive. *The next job's gonna fall on me? Yeah, right. Fuck that.* The next job's gonna be *by me*, more likely. *Imagine that shit,* he groused mentally, *drove here from Mott Street? To chew my ass?*

Fuck that, fuck that, fuck that, kept banging on his ear.

Taking a deep breath, he calmed himself.

He kept the Rado, but bundled away the rest of the watches under the floorboards beneath the Job Lot wall mirror. When he eyed his reflection, he liked what he saw and paused in the shadows to admire his own nakedness. Almost five-foot ten, he had a body like Bruce Lee, but on steroids, and a face that could have starred in movies in Hong Kong. Handsome in a cool way. A lover *and* a fighter. It was because of all the women in his life, he smirked into the mirror. What facial hair he had amounted to a faint mustache and goatee, which he trimmed regularly because he knew the ladies liked it. And the ladies: Mimi at the New Wave Salon, who permed his hair, and shaped it according to pictures in Hong Kong movie-star magazines. Joanna, his dentist, who'd given him a winning smile. Angela, the seamstress who fixed his jackets, and who'd made it clear she wanted to get into his pants. Dana, the masseuse, who

103

pampered his muscles, including the long one that hung loose beneath his stomach. Kitty, at the bank, who gave him the crisp new bills he liked. On and on. Women were taken in by his good looks, his dynamic energy, and his quick tongue. Some of the women would later appreciate his quick tongue in more earthy ways.

He heard the *dailo*'s voice again and shook his head, remembering the Jung Wah Warehouse job. *That* job was mostly the Jung brothers, who had hot-wired the truck inside the warehouse after Shorty had wriggled inside and let them in. They drove off with the entire load, with Shorty locking up the warehouse neatly, and Koo Jai covering shotgun on the rip-off. *But abalone and bird's-nests?* They'd unloaded the stuff to the Jung brothers' cousins who operated a market in Boston Chinatown, but they hadn't seen any money yet. *What the fuck?* It would be weeks, maybe months. He'd thought it was a stupid heist but went along to give the Jung brothers face.

He went to the table and took a gulp from the bottle of mouthwash there, gargled, and ejected the green spew into a plastic garbage pail. Thinking it might be better to cool his plan to rob the Fuk's mahjong club, he sucked out the rinse where it leached into his gums and spat again. The old floorboards still creaked under the dingy linoleum, even after he'd covered it with cheap area rugs from Kmart.

From the back room he could hear the rustling of the comforter, then a soft murmur, like a sigh. He went toward the musty heat, the Rado in one hand, his cock in the other as he thought about Tina, lying exhausted but insatiable in his bed.

She was the night manager at KK's Karaoke, a basement spot on Allen Street. Koo Jai had done her several times and he knew she hoped to be his girlfriend, even thought she could get rid of the others.

He slipped under the comforter, in the darkness behind the drawn shades, feeling for her. He put the Rado on her wrist, and she moaned, thinking, *Not the handcuffs again.*

Koo Jai nuzzled the nape of her neck, his cold hard body sucking the heat from the comforter and the hot contours of her backside.

"Ooooh," she moaned, so cool. She turned and nestled all of her soft and wet parts against him. Admiring the Rado, she slipped her head down to his stomach and wrapped her hot lips around the thick popsicle there.

He watched the tangle of hair pumping back and forth on his *lun* cock, and wondered how long before he could rob the mahjong club.

Payoff

Bo crossed the Bowery toward the long blocks of jewelry stores that ran down the northside stretch of Canal Street. Fifty shops named Treasure Diamonds, Lucky Star Jewelry, Royal Princess, Golden Jade, Canal National Gems, with the lights blazing from their windows brightening the concrete gray gloom drifting west toward the Holland Tunnel.

She always made her payments on the first Sunday morning of every month, as soon as the stores opened, so she wouldn't be delayed by other customers.

Almost to Mulberry Street, she paused at the bulletproof

glass door of Foo Ling Jewelry and Jade, and waited to be buzzed in.

The Foo Ling's street windows displayed a dazzling array of diamond rings, bracelets, necklaces, and custom setups mounted with rubies or emeralds, all gleaming under the brilliant halogen lights. There were trays of gold medallions, racks of thick glittering chains, and a section of rich green jade pieces, some carved and beaded into pendants.

She stepped into the dry heat spreading from the lights, went past the display counters along the walls.

The bald-headed old Chinese man sat alone in the back end of the store, his fat bottom propped against a wooden stool. He twisted his frown into a half-sneer, half-smile, removing his finger from the remote door button as he watch Bo approach. Her eyes avoided his.

Hom Sook was how she was first introduced to him, her contact for remitting the monthly payments, and that was how she addressed him regularly now, always reminded how the spoken Chinese words sounded like *hom sup,* horny, old lech.

The name fit him well, she thought.

Hom Sook was sixtyish, obese, and reeked of the pork dumplings and curry chicken that he loved so much. He had a big head with reptilian features: thin lips, hooded eyes, and a flat nose.

Bo pictured this snakehead each time she prepared her payment envelope.

This time he'd worn the cheap gray rayon shirt with a design of tigers and eagles dueling in the background. He smirked, leering at her, when she handed him the envelope of money.

Bo had always kept the exchange brief, waiting just long

enough to see him make the notation. She didn't want to engage him in conversation, knowing where it would lead.

"*Leng nui,*" he called her, pretty woman. " You look tired," he said in a slithery voice. "How are things with you?"

"Fine," Bo answered evenly. "Thank you."

"Have you reconsidered our offer?" he asked, the snake tongue licking his lips.

They had wanted her to whore for them, had promised her a choice of regulars, clean-cut family men who were easy to please. *Easy work,* they'd said. *Money for laying on your back.*

"No, thank you," Bo repeated as he counted out the money, then made a notation in his black book. Seeing this, Bo turned for the door. The old lech swallowed back his lust, his eyes keening to the soft sway of her backside as he made her pause before buzzing her out.

"*Leng nui,*" he chortled, "see you next month."

Outside the Foo Ling, Bo took a deep breath, welcoming the cold breeze that swept down Canal. She felt better as she walked, thinking of a small sunny village in the south of China, picturing her daughter and her mother there, half a world and three lifetimes away.

Time and Space

Bo sat in the quiet solitude of her little rented room above Market Street, the silence broken only by the clicking of her bamboo needles, seated at the foot edge of the single bed, her voice a whisper chanting Buddhist *nom mor nom mor* prayers.

She continued knitting this version of her rosary, a black scarf with the Chinese words for struggle, *jung jot,* stitched across the top in white relief.

In the black yarn were all the colors of bad luck.

In the white yarn, absent color, the insidious tone of death.

She was playing off the bad luck.

Several inches below the Chinese characters was a repeating pattern of horizontal S's, or white snakes. Two rows of them totaling twenty-five, now twenty-six with the one she was stitching in place.

Twenty-six snakes now. Twenty-six payments to the snakeheads.

She paused, and took a breath, let her eyes rove over the bowl of leftover *jik sik,* instant ramen, on a tray, over the top of the used dresser, to the grainy photograph of three women: herself, and Mother, and small daughter in tow.

Only the child was smiling.

The little girl's mother and grandmother wore uncertainty on their faces, had small lights of hope and resignation in their eyes.

Abruptly, Bo wrenched her attention back to the clicking needles, clicking faster now, left to right, an impatient rhythm.

She hadn't seen them in more than a year, but they spoke every week, using the discount prepaid telephone calling cards that Sai Go had gotten for her.

Nom mor nom mor nom or may tor fut.

She focused on the needles working the yarn: slip, stitch, purl, her fingers, hands, wrists in active articulation. The same energy came from her hands when she'd cut Sai Go's hair, massaged his shoulders.

The black acrylic scarf was almost two feet long, knitted in monthly installments of white snakes.

She prayed for strength to finish it, knowing it would take years before she'd be able to pay off the snakeheads.

Nom mor nom mor no more slip stitch, loop through, the ball of yarn twisting in the little plastic basket. Drop the white yarn, wrap the black, complete stitch.

In the back of her mind she remembered the myriad of forgotten jobs, and then the New Canton, and measured the price of freedom.

Secret Society

Gee Sin rolled down the middle window of the van just a crack, then leaned back and sipped his steaming *nai cha* as he observed the area around the foot of the Manhattan Bridge.

The generic gray minivan with dark-tinted windows was parked off Division Street, providing him with cover against wind or rain, with a good view of East Broadway where Forsyth Street reached up to Chrystie Park.

Gee Sin could see the rows of businesses beneath the high bridge girders: several storefront employment agencies, Chinese vendors with outdoor ATM machines, a MoneyGram shop, and a Western Union at either end of the street. On the opposite block was a hole-in-the-wall store that sold cell phones and prepaid telephone cards flanked by a fruit stand and a stall that sold socks and thermal underwear, toothbrushes and soap, necessities for newly arrived Chinese who were about to travel yet again.

Things had been set up just the way they'd planned, Gee Sin thought. Made it convenient to find work, get cash, and remit payments. Cell phones and prepaid cards to call home regularly, and be reminded about their debts.

The steam from the cup swirled toward the sliver of open window, as he felt a quick sweep of icy wind across his bald pate. The intersection was noisy and crowded this early afternoon. The bundled people shuddered under the thunder of the subway trains overhead. The only dialect he heard was Fukienese.

Gee Sin was pleased to see the streets in this area were wider, able to accommodate sweeping turns, and the stretch of streets along Chrystie Park allowed a dozen buses to park there.

There was a Mobil gas station at the corner of Allen. He'd arranged a cash-only gas-up deal with the franchise owner for the overnight buses that parked along Pike Street. His scheme for the Hung Huen was about to bear fruit. The triad, washing money, had arranged for the financing of a fleet of coach buses, two dozen to start. Since many of the riders would be Fukienese, the Fuk Chow gang would run the daily operations.

Gee Sin, or *Paper Fan*, as the triad members respectfully addressed him, had orchestrated every step. He had seen how important the American expansion of the Chinese restaurant industry was. As more and more Chinese restaurants, take-out shops, and *dim sum* teahouses flourished in far-flung American cities, the demand for cheap Chinese-speaking labor also grew. Entrepreneurs had even demanded that certain tong-connected construction crews be transported to the locale of the new restaurant, to be housed and fed there as they built—and inflated—the costs of the business.

The Fukienese, the latest wave to fill the demand for coolie workers, were sent to restaurants and malls from Richmond to Rochester, as far west as Ohio, and north to Montreal.

Twelve dollars one-way to Boston or Philadelphia would drive any competition out.

The idea that they needed a transportation system to shuttle these workers back and forth from New York's Chinatown, the hub, made Gee Sin realize that the unregulated tour-bus business was also a natural for moving contraband along the interstates.

A patrol car cruised by.

He adjusted the cup in his hand, placed it into the slide-out cup holder between the front seats. From his pocket he fished out a bogus driver's license the triad had created for him. The name they'd used was Bok Ji Fan, another version of *White Paper Fan.* He studied the photograph with a sad knowing smile. The weight of fifty years sagged around his eyes, the brows bushy and flecked with gray. He stared out of deep-set, sunken eyes within a haunted, pale face. He reminded himself that there was much to do, and his time in America was short. He was not one who was keen on travel; the month away from Hong Kong was long enough already.

As White Paper Fan, he'd gotten accustomed to the creature comforts of Hong Kong that accorded his rank and seniority in the Red Circle.

New York was nothing but cold and gray grit.

Gee Sin thought about the triad's Grass Sandal rank liaison officer who would drive them back to the rented condo apartment outside Chinatown. Scanning the street, he saw a bus discharge its passengers and head toward the park, exhaust pouring from its tailpipe. From a side street, a line of black funeral cars swept past him. He was glad to see the bad luck spirits fade into the avenue.

He checked his watch again, confident Grass Sandal would arrive soon. The street was productive, which was all he'd wanted to see. He pocketed the fake license, then picked up the cup, sipped the tea carefully, and watched traffic as he shut the window with his free hand.

Watch Out

Koo Jai sat upright in his bed and reached across for the lady's watch, a gold and black Rado nestled in the soft hollows of his thick comforter, where it had landed after Tina flung it at him in a fit of jealous fury. She'd finally realized that his other girlfriends weren't going to disappear.

Fuck that little cunt. He grinned to himself; there'd be another piece of ass soon enough, another quickie conquest. Any village girl out of the Guangjo backwater, who'd never seen better than a Timex, would surely give it all up for the diamond-speckled watch. *Why do I waste my time on jealous bitches anyway?* he asked himself.

He placed the Rado on the metal folding table and leaned back against the pillows. He drained the last of the bottle of Tsingtao beer and was considering opening another when there was a knock on the door.

Tina, he thought, *coming back to beg forgiveness.* Maybe he'd let her suck his cock if she was truly repentant.

Another knock, and then Shorty's voice froze him

"Koo," Shorty called, "open up."

Strange, Koo Jai thought, pulling his pistol from beneath the pillows as he quietly stepped toward the front door.

"Shorty?" he replied. "You alone?"

"No," Shorty answered.

"Open up!" demanded a second voice he instantly recognized as belonging to the *dailo.*

But here? Now? Why? Koo Jai shook off the panic, shoved the gun under the sofa cushions, then reached for the door.

Lucky smirked at the sight of Koo Jai in his black briefs.

Kongo stepped inside, tossing two cartons of cigarettes and a bag of pills onto the sofa as Shorty backed into the room, followed by Lucky.

Koo Jai moved away from the door.

Lucky spotted the butt of the pistol protruding from beneath the cushion. "*Kai dai,* punk." He grinned. "You expecting trouble?"

"No," answered Koo Jai, still confused by the surprise visit. "It's just that no one ever comes up here."

"Right." Lucky snickered. "Just you and the *leng nui,* the pretty girls. "

Kongo stood between the sofa and Koo Jai, letting his duster hang open to show the scattergun hanging by his side. Lucky threw Shorty Ng a hard look, saying, "Take a walk. Check the park for Fuks and come back in ten minutes."

Shorty glanced at Koo Jai, before squeezing past Kongo, relieved to escape from the overheated room.

Sensing Koo Jai's confusion, Lucky said, "Relax. The smokes and the pills are for you boys out here. Something to keep you going while you're watching the streets, especially near the park." Lucky stepped to the front window, checked the view on East Broadway.

"Why? What's up?" asked Koo Jai.

"I want you all to keep an eye on the street where the Chinese buses are parked."

The puzzled look stayed on Koo Jai's face.

Lucky said, "See if any Fuks are hanging around. Are they getting on the buses? Or following in their cars? Or are they just putting muscle on the street?"

"Can't you tell me what's coming down?" Koo Jai asked, pulling on his pants.

"Don't ask so many fuckin' questions," Lucky warned. "And don't forget, we still want the motherfuckers who been robbing our members." He turned toward the back of the apartment. "Whaddya got back there? That the love nest?"

Koo Jai followed Lucky to his bedroom, the heavy footsteps of Kongo behind him.

"Shit, it's hot as hell back here," Lucky said.

"Makes the girls take their clothes off faster," Koo Jai deadpanned.

Lucky noticed the black-faced and diamond Rado, lifted it from the folding table.

"Nice," he said. "I know just the girl for this. You don't mind, right?"

Koo Jai shook his head as Lucky pocketed the watch.

"It's Christmastime, you know."

Koo Jai nodded, keeping the smile on his face.

Lucky grinned at stone-faced Kongo. "Maybe I'll get lucky, huh?" He laughed at his own joke, continuing, "Or maybe *she'll* get Lucky."

Kongo kept his eyes on Koo Jai as they left the apartment.

"Keep watching," barked Lucky. "And keep that fuckin' cell phone on."

Koo Jai closed the door and listened to the sound of their footsteps thumping down the stairs. He sat on the sofa and retrieved his gun, suspicion in his heart about the change in the *dailo*'s demeanor. He felt suddenly thirsty, and tried to find clarity in another bottle of Tsingtao.

Kongo led the way out of the tenement. Lucky squeezed the Rado in the sweaty palm of his big hand as they came onto East Broadway. They headed for the black Buick, Lucky thinking, *Lee's watches,* wondering if Skinny Chin took better care of his list of serial numbers than he did of his merchandise.

White and Red

The Ecstasy sharpened his instincts, Lucky felt, but the more he took, the more he needed to get the same bounce. Now the *ma huang* and his instincts were bracing him up.

Gray light in late afternoon. The streets looked slippery, under a mushy white coating. He passed over the Gucci loafers, thinking how streetwise he was, and laced up the black steel-toed Doc Martens with the rubber traction soles.

Imagining himself in a fight, he raised his hands in a Wing Chun–style pose, striking a sloppy cat-stance. The loose-fitting carpenter jeans puffed up where extra pockets held a box cutter, a cell phone.

He popped another one of the red pills and washed it down with a chug of Grey Goose from a pint-sized bottle, a taste from the twenty cases they'd taken from Fook Lau Liquors.

Another gambling debt squared up and then some.

He sensed he should press the element of surprise, and ambush Koo Jai again. Kongo was holed up in a catnap with some Malay ho, and Lefty, fighting off a hangover from the free vodka, had crashed in the clubhouse.

Go alone this time, pull off a bluff, see what turns up.

He walked over to East Broadway, kept his gun hand near the nine in his pocket as he stepped up and knocked on Koo Jai's door.

No answer.

He punched up Koo Jai's pager, standing there quietly but heard only silence from within. He knocked again, waited another minute before going back down the stairs. At the rear of the street landing, he checked the fire escapes above him, didn't see any movement there.

Head toward the far end, he was thinking, as he turned down East Broadway.

People on the street were hustling to buy their dinner groceries as the weather worsened. The fish vendors were barking at their customers, threatening to close shop. Lucky looked in the direction of Pike Street, intuiting that Koo Jai had gone that way. Halfway down the dark street he saw a skelly-looking white man outside the local methadone clinic, bobbing and weaving in the middle of the slushy sidewalk, forcing Chinese *ah por*, grandmothers, to shift their bags of *choy*, and walk around him.

Lucky brushed him with his shoulder as he passed.

In his junkie haze the man muttered just loud enough for Lucky to hear the words *chinky shit . . .*

Lucky took a few more steps and stopped suddenly, as if he remembered something, then turned, bringing his hands up as if he were adjusting sunglasses, stepping toward the man. An arm's length away, Lucky leaned forward and drove the heel of his open right palm full force into the man's chin. Shock crossed the man's face, hate tearing up in his eyes as he tasted his own poisoned blood oozing from the dangling piece of tongue he'd bitten off. That froze him for the two seconds it took for Lucky to kick his heel through the man's knee, feeling the ligaments give way like rotted rubber bands as he started to fall forward. Lucky grabbed him by his collar and twisted him so that he dove headlong into concrete and steel steps, spewing what looked like bloody kernels of corn from his mouth. Lucky swung a vicious kick with the steel-toed boot into the man's ribs. The junkie mutt choked and started to vomit.

That good enough? Lucky roared inside his head, *that enough fuckin' chinky shit for you, hah?* He wiped the slime off the Doc Martens, dragging his feet through the dirty slush as he left the scene, cursing as he went.

He could see flashing lights in the distance, too far away to tell if that meant cops, or emergency workers. At the corner, he changed direction. His Ecstasy-driven bravado was crashing.

He considered his options as the rotating lights got closer, and grudgingly turned back toward the Bayard Street condo.

It was Koo Jai, he thought, who was the *lucky* one tonight.

Sin

Grass Sandal had chosen the location well. The new condo-minium high-rise, Tribeca West, had been one of the Red Circle's Manhattan real-estate investments, another opportunity to *sai chien*, to wash its dirty money. The condo stood at the edge of Hudson Square, conveniently near the Holland Tunnel and the Westside Highway if a need to escape the city arose. Since the building was only half occupied, Gee Sin's movements would arouse little attention. He poured himself a tumbler of XO brandy and stepped out on to the dark balcony, thinking that the colorful lights across the river reminded him of Hong Kong. The Red Circle's plans were in place, and besides the fleet of buses, other arrangements had already been set in motion.

The wind whipped up suddenly, and he went back inside, put the tumbler down. He looked around and was pleased: simple furnishings, all rented, so the triad would not be stuck, money tied up in idle property. The condo unit could be cleared on short notice and made available for sale.

All the Red Circle's investments in Manhattan properties

had been successful, and real-estate prices continued to rise.

Gee Sin went to the walk-in closet and tapped in the code numbers to the wall safe hidden there. From the safe he extracted stacks of plastic cards, then proceeded to the living room. In that quiet space, under the flood of light from a solitary overhead pendant lamp, he squared up the decks of plastic on the black-stone slab surface that separated the dining from the living areas. He dealt the cards out with his left hand, the blank plastic flashing smoothly between thumb and trigger finger, sliding out from the flick of the wrist.

Nine piles of eleven cards each. He shuffled them into neat stacks, three across, three down.

The *black* Visa card blanks, across the top. *Black, the color of night, the shade of secrecy, the black of the hak se wui,* secret societies.

The *gold* American Express cards. *Wong,* yellow, in the middle of everything.

And the Platinum MasterCard blanks.

Gold and silver, very much favored by the Chinese.

He took another swallow from the glass of brandy, caught his breath, and closed his eyes. They had learned quickly from past operations. Instead of selling the cards to amateurs who would get caught and call attention to the operators, he'd decided to use selected Chinese people in order to impose control and improve communication. The idea of using storage locations and closed warehouses was his way of gaining mobility and volume for the operators.

They would fence the products through the triad's legitimate businesses.

When he opened his eyes, he saw the array of stacks differently. They were ghost identities, cards ready to be imprinted

119

with a rotating selection of Chinese names: Chins and Changs, Dongs, Fongs, and Gongs, and a lot of Lees and Wongs.

Stolen account numbers would be loaded onto the magnetic strip of the blank. The Chinese name would be matched to a recruited shopper, whose picture had been taken for a bogus driver's license for picture identification. The fake licenses, computer-generated, were virtually undistinguishable from the real deal. Any of the mobile mills, with portable laptops and rented laser printers, could turn out acceptable forged passports and visas as well.

They'd refined forgery, fraudulent credit, and identity theft into an art *and* a science.

He reflected on the society's Thirty-Six Strategies. He'd added a twist to Number Seven, *Create something out of nothing, to use false information effectively.* They were creating false identities, welding real account numbers to paper names, breeding phantoms who would bring millions to the Red Circle. *To steal the dragon and replace it with the phoenix,* steal account numbers and supply them with new faces.

It had begun with the Red Circle's number forty-nines—*sai gow jai,* dog soldiers—who'd kidnapped an Asia Bank One executive in Vancouver, B.C., and managed to rip off a delivery of credit-card machines. The scam operations had worked well on a small scale at first, but now they were spreading east and west via Canadian Chinatowns.

Gee Sin would introduce the fraudulent organizations to America.

He felt proud, marveled at how smoothly everything fit together, how each scam unit found its way around the Fukienese, the latest wave of Chinese immigrants. They became fodder for the ever-expanding Chinese restaurant business, suckers for Chinese loan sharks, and desperadoes to enlist in the credit-card operation. The tour buses only made it easier for all the crews to move around. Paper Fan had foreseen that the buses connecting the many restaurants among the triads' dues-paying members, transporting the Fukienese filling in as kitchen help, deported to far-flung kitchens in this strange *gwai* devil land, could be the basis for a network. Hung Huen card operators trolled the Fukienese employment agencies for unemployed Chinese willing to participate in fraud. The crews of recruiters, under Grass Sandal's instructions, also kept an eye on the Chinese gamblers, high rollers, at the casinos in Atlantic City, and at Foxwoods and Mohegan Sun as well, hunting for players who needed cash.

In addition, some of the Chinese restaurants yielded disgruntled employees who sold customer's credit-card information to the triad, ten dollars for each account. The *sai gow jai* collected the information, and the tech mills manufactured the bogus driver's licenses to match the fake cards. Underpaid salespeople at cell-phone shops and dishonest bank clerks sold clients' personal information, too. The sweeper at a video-rental store might provide a hundred confidential application forms. There was no shortage of illegal immigrants at the ends of their ropes, convenient bodies with which to create new accounts. When the accounts were maxed out, the body would disappear to another forsaken kitchen in the hinterlands. If they got caught, Immigration gave them a free ticket back to China.

Gee Sin, the mastermind, took advantage of the Americans' holiday preoccupation with gift giving, the annual buying frenzy that overwhelmed what was originally a religious holiday.

Paper Fan realized how important these several weeks were to merchants, hoping to make sales to carry them through the year, which in the crazed crush of business made them careless and blind to credit-card fraud.

The bogus cards would be automatically approved by the retailer's swipe-reader because the account number was legitimate. If the store required photo identification, there was the fake driver's license that provided it. Cashiers readily accepted the machine's approval, especially when faced with a long line of tired shoppers waiting to pay. During the holidays, credit-account spending levels normally scrutinized were relaxed, and high-end purchases were less likely to be questioned.

The Chinese *shoppers* had been instructed to buy certain brand-name merchandise, popular items that would be easy to move.

He took another taste of the brandy and his vision of the plastic decks changed again. Now he saw an array of Chinese communities inside American cities, each one under the influence of triad clans and tong-affiliated gangs. The three stacks on the right were Boston, New York, New Jersey. They'd partnered with the Fuk Chow on the East Coast. The three stacks on the left were the West Coast cities of Seattle, San Francisco, and Los Angeles. The Suey Ching ran the northern two, but the Viet Ching controlled the cards in L.A., and were tops in Texas Chinatowns as well. The middle decks were Columbus/Cleveland, Philadelphia, and Richmond/Norfolk. The Sun Wo clan worked the cards in all those mid-American cities.

Besides dispatching Fukinese desperadoes to scam the local merchants, Gee Sin advised Grass Sandal to select the best English-speaking recruits to work the phones against the mail-order companies, directing Christmas gift merchandise to a series of storage facilities and shuttered storefronts. At these locations, designated triad officers with bogus identification would await the deliverymen and sign for the items. The phone-scam operators focused on high-end electronics that the Red Circle could sell easily through its network of merchants, expensive items like video camcorders, digital cameras, Walkmen and laptop computers.

They'd expected to steal several million dollars of merchandise over the holidays, all through fraudulent credit-card transactions. The legitimate account holder and the card-issuing company wouldn't detect anything amiss until weeks after the holidays, when the monthly statements arrived in the mail. By then, Paper Fan and his operatives would be long gone, leaving only a trail of smoke and shadows.

His thoughts changed again as he felt a slow dull throbbing at his wrist, and he leaned back away from the stacks of cards. Occasionally he'd feel a sharp pain at the wrist. This occurred mostly in winter or in cold locations like Vancouver or Toronto, where he had first tested the credit-card operations.

Time to take it off, he thought.

The psychiatric member of the rehabilitation and therapy team at Kowloon had suggested to him the idea of *residual pain,* the severed nerves remembering the moment of the chop. *It's all in the brain,* she'd said, *you think you feel pain so you do feel pain.* Mostly it was chafing, or too much pressure at the new joint, where scar-sealed bone and muscle bumped against the silicone-padded socket of the prosthesis.

He could remove the prosthesis to relieve the pain. Pain-killer medication was prescribed.

Dew keuih, fuck, he cursed quietly. He knew it wasn't the hand. It fit well and he'd trained on it, and *willed* it to work well. *It wasn't the hand.*

It was the attack that he remembered, hazy but still horrific even after twenty-five years. The pain of a young man revived in the stump arm of an old man.

The glint of light from his left. Raising his bow arm reflexively. It wasn't the hand, marvelously sculpted and engineered.

He'd been knocked down. When he braced to get up he saw that he had no left hand.

It was the memory.

And he had survived the attack. The chop had been intented for his neck.

He detached the elastic and Velcro band that wrapped around his elbow, and slipped the hand off, placing it on the black marble. It always looked strange, removed from his arm, especially when he walked further from it, and viewed his hand in the near distance. His real hand felt like reaching for it.

He imagined it as a weapon, the sling its holster.

Touch

Already five years old, the bionic hand was an ultralite model, a myoelectric prosthesis with articulate fingers, an opposable thumb, a rotating wrist. It was powered by batteries inside the fake limb. Sensors there detected when the arm muscles contracted, then converted the body's electrical signal into electric power. This powered the motor controlling the hand and wrist, its skeletal frame made of thermoplastics and titanium for extreme flexibility. The frame was covered with a skin of silicone that was resistant to heat and flame, and custom colored to match the patient's skin pigmentation. The hand and fingers were sculpted with fingernails, knuckles, and creases. At a glance, it was indistinguishable from a real hand.

It cost eighty thousand dollars in Hong Kong and the triad had paid without question.

Removing it from his arm reminded him of the rehabilitation course at the Kowloon Clinic, where he'd trained to use his new artificial limb. He'd continued for a year until his control of hand and finger movements became so deft that he could eat with chopsticks, and deal a deck of cards. He could pluck a coin off the table.

He could pull the trigger of a gun.

Aaya, he sighed, remembering the first of the Thirty-Six Strategies of the society, *cross the ocean without letting the sky know.* Of course, he was here to oversee the tour buses and the credit cards, but—known only to himself and the *dragonhead,* leader of the triad—there was the matter of the missing diamonds and gold Panda coins in the wake of the Uncle Four murder, not to mention a hundred thousand in Hip Ching cash stolen from the foolish old man by his vengeful mistress. Uncle Four had been en route to a meeting with Hakka heroin dealers before he was murdered. His mistress had disappeared.This was not something they could suffer quietly, even though much of what was missing was swag. Before returning to Hong Kong, he knew he'd have to look into the situation. He took a Vicodin pill, washing it down with the last of the liquor. After a minute he lay down and let go of the progressions in his head. The room went black and he dreamed he was flying, watching the landforms below, marking his way back to the fragrant harbor of Hong Kong.

Crime No Holiday

Pearl Harbor memorials had reminded Jack of Pa's Japanese nightmares.

Then the nights had run together and suddenly it was late December. Senior detectives had pulled holiday time, so he'd been reassigned to cover the four to midnight.

Christmas Eve.

It didn't matter much to Jack. He didn't have family plans or commitments like most of the other detectives.

Coming out of the Tofu King with his steaming quart of *dao jeung,* bean milk, Jack headed toward the Bowery, thinking about hooking up with Billy for a few holiday drinks after his shift. There wasn't a bus in sight, so he decided to walk north through Chinatown, hoping to catch a cab somewhere along the way back to the 0-9.

Many of the restaurants and stores hung gaily-colored strands of Christmas-tree lights in their windows, not out of tradition but as eye candy to attract the tourist dollar. Those businesses that were heavily supported by neighborhood Chinese—the coffee shops, bakeries, barbershops, and grocery stores—didn't bother to decorate, knowing that the *real* decorating time would come during the Chinese New Year, when the brilliant reds and golds of luck and prosperity would appear everywhere.

Farther out on Fukienese East Broadway it felt even less like Christmas, no trace of religion or pretense of tradition there. On some of those streets it didn't seem like New York, or even America.

Like somewhere in a foreign port.

Only the American-born Chinese, derisively referred to by "real" Chinese as *jook-sings,* the empty pieces of bamboo, had absorbed enough of the American Christmas tradition to put up Christmas trees in their homes, to exchange holiday cards and gifts. Jack remembered that Pa had refused to allow a tree into their tenement flat, saying it was a fire hazard, the apartment was too small, and the pine needles would make an unholy mess.

Jack went past Eldridge, where the discount greengrocer's makeshift marketplace bumped up against the coach buses at the curb, everyone hustling to make a buck. Everybody watching everybody else. At Delancey, he finally caught a packed northbound M 103 bus, and rode it the ten blocks into the Ninth Precinct. The *dao jeung* had chilled, but he knew he could nuke it in the stationhouse's microwave.

He got off on Fifth and went east into the black afternoon.

Xmas Eve

The news on the radio in the squad room was predicting snow and traffic delays. When Jack reviewed the blotter, he saw there was a rash of shoplifting incidents, and credit-card fraud. Blacks and Latinos boosting their gift lists. Chinese names on bogus credit cards. *Merry Christmas,* he thought sardonically, *by any means necessary.*

He sipped the *dao jeung* he'd zapped in the microwave.

Happy holidays all, as he scrolled down the listings, an unending litany of petty larcenies.

Six hours into the shift, the foot of snow outside resulted in squad cars and scooters parked at odd angles. From the window by the restrooms, Jack could see how quickly the thick flurries were falling, heavily enough so that he could barely make out the colors of traffic lights and street signs at the intersection. *A nasty night to be out.*

A call came in from the cold. He could hear the beating of the wind against the caller's mouthpiece when he flipped open his cell phone, a dull, broken static accompanying rushing noise.

"Sarge told me to call you . . ." P.O. Wong was saying, something about a *takeout, missing persons,* and just before the call went dead, *deliveryman.*

Jack hit redial, got nothing.

It took him by surprise. Not that the call came on his cell phone, or that it was P.O. Wong, but because it was the late shift and Wong worked the eight to four, days. He figured Wong to be homefree, enjoying the holiday evening, by now.

Jack finished the last of the warm bean milk.

Then the desk phone rang, a call transferred from the front by the officer on duty.

P.O. Wong again. "I'm calling from a bodega on Seventh . . ."

"Much better," Jack answered.

"Here's the deal," Wong continued. "I just finished a twelve-hour pull. Sarge says there's no more holiday OT, so I'm on my own time here."

"Okay. So?"

"So nine-one-one caught some frantic calls from a Chinese speaker, they think. Had problems with the language. The other portables on the job caught two domestic beefs, one by the park, the other in the yuppie condos by Lafayette. Sarge is tied up with some D&D's from the college bars. It's a mess."

"And it's Christmas Eve to boot," Jack added, not surprised that people got drunk, or that domestic disputes boiled over especially during the holidays, proving how frail and screwed-up people were, fighting over such seemingly small and insignificant crap.

"Right," continued Wong, "so the frantic calls are coming from the New Golden Chinatown over on Tenth, that's One-Nine-Nine East Tenth. When I called, the woman said her son went out on deliveries and hasn't returned. She's crying because he's long overdue. That was before my cell died."

There was a pause, something Spanish in the background, *chino-chino, maricon,* then laughter.

"The house wants to treat it like a Missing Persons," Wong continued. "That means waiting to see if he shows up because of whatever reason. But the mother's freaking out."

Jack knew it wasn't his call to tell a rookie cop to do the right thing, above and beyond, all that.

But Wong said it for him. "I'm on my own time but I thought I'd give it a look-see before going home. What do you think?"

It wasn't a homicide call, and Jack knew, in a city where you could get killed for the way you looked at someone, for the colors you wore, or over a parking spot, or an imagined slight, or for just having the bad luck to be in the wrong place at the wrong time, *that* killer call could hit the precinct at any moment. But at *this* moment no homicide cases were piling onto his desk, and it being a Chinese thing, Jack knew the house would like to have him involved. Any important calls could be patched to his cell anyway.

"Let's go over together," Jack heard himself saying, "to at least get the story straight. Maybe it's nothing, I wrap it up, and you can go home. One ninety-nine? I'll meet you there." He hung up, but remembered he'd agreed to meet Alexandra for the Christmas Eve Candlelight Service at midnight, an uplifting Mass at the Church of True Light in Chinatown. If anything. . . he'd give her a heads-up.

And there was Billy who'd be hanging out at Grampa's, ready to partake in some holiday drinking. *No worries there.*

Happy Family

Jack stepped out of the warm stationhouse into the bracing gusts of wind that whipped in from the East River. He couldn't help feeling dread; the fear that the frantic call would be serious juiced up his adrenaline.

He blew out a steamy billowing breath, cursed quietly, and began the cold trudge toward East Tenth.

The New Golden Chinatown was a hole-in-the-wall take-out joint near the northern edge of Alphabet City. The snow-covered awning announced Hunan Szechuan Cantonese cuisine and in bold letters EAT IN TAKE OUT.

Crossing the street Jack could see the glaring fluorescent light spilling out, a bright menu board with a series of color shots of food dishes running the length of the ceiling above a pass-through counter area. *What you see is what you get.*

There was a bicycle chained to the rollgate railing. Jack could tell a place was successful by the number of locked-up bicycles out front. This run-down kitchen was a two-bike operation, nothing big, barely enough take-out deliveries to make ends meet.

He paused at the door and saw a Chinese man and woman talking to P.O. Wong, who was taking notes on a pocket notepad. Jack scanned the operation: pink-tiled walls, some big woks in the dark kitchen at the rear. Two shallow counters that ran along the short side wall and then across the street window. A big garbage bin. There were no chairs and tables so it was clear they didn't want people hanging around. *Eat and go.* There was a cashier's area set off behind greasy panels of bulletproof Plexiglas. *You bought your food the same way you'd buy rotgut at a ghetto liquor store, like cashing your paper in a low-rent check-cashing shack.*

The woman, in her forties, was animated, and the man, probably also in his forties but looking older, was trying to maintain his control, concern etched onto their tired faces. Jack could see how the grinding restaurant hours had worn them down, years they'd never get back, a generation of sacrifice for their little piece of the American Dream, the *Gum San* gold mountain dream.

Jack pushed open the fractured glass door and was hit by the smell of grease and salt in the steamy air. They turned toward him and he flashed his badge right away to alleviate any fears, gaving the couple a polite nod. They had been speaking a kind of Fukienese Mandarin from which P.O. Wong was piecing together the situation. Their teenage son, Hong, about five-foot six, wearing a gray jacket with hood, and black jeans, had gone out on deliveries and hadn't returned. Calls to his cell phone went unanswered.

"Where's the order pad?" asked Jack.

P.O. Wong handed it over, and as Jack scanned the addresses, Wong said, "There were two deliveries, one on Twelfth, the other over by the river at the Riis Houses.

"If only Ah Jun hadn't called out sick," the father groaned, "Hong wouldn't have had to help out today. He had hoped to go to a party after work."

"Maybe he went straight to the party? After making the deliveries?"

"No, never. He would have called. His cell phone—"

"He had trouble with that phone," the mother interrupted. "The battery was bad, and the service was unreliable."

P.O. Wong, considering that his own cell phone had just died, said, "Maybe he tried to call?"

"Could he have gone to the party, planning to call you when he got there?" offered Jack.

"No," they both answered. " He's not like that. He's a good boy, responsible. Top student in school."

"We wanted to close up," fretted the father. "Not just because of the weather, but also because it's Christmas, and it's a family night. We were ready to go home." He exchanged a stunned look with his wife, adding softly, "But then the two orders came in . . ." She looked away and started trembling as he continued, "They totaled over ninety dollars. We couldn't turn them down, a twenty-minute cook and pack." He paused, took a breath. "Then the delivery. If everything goes okay, we go home before eleven."

The father looked from Jack to P.O. Wong, and back. "But then we got the orders. . . ," he repeated, putting his arm across his wife's shoulder.

Jack saw telephone numbers scrawled across the top of the order pad. The last two deliveries were far apart; the first was to 129 Twelfth Street, for Stenhagen. *Shrimp with Snow Peas, mixed Vegetables, Seafood Delight.* Sounded like NYU people. Twenty-three dollars and a free can of no-name cola. The second delivery was to 444 Avenue D, at the river's edge of the Alphabets, in the Jacob Riis Houses, deep into the projects. To a Miller, Das, something-scribbled, apartment 14D. A large order, doubles on everything: General Tso's Chicken, Mongolian Beef, Happy Family Combo, and four quarts of fried rice and lo mein. Almost seventy dollars. *A projects party or a group with mad holiday munchies.*

P.O. Wong jotted down the last statements. The mother had continued to call the son's cell phone. And they had tried calling the order numbers back, to track deliveries, but the first customer hung up when she was unable to understand their poor English. The second number never answered and their call went to a voice-mail blank.

"According to Dad here," Wong offered, "both deliveries should have taken a total of a half hour, forty minutes tops. And now we're a half hour on top of that."

"What does the bike look like?" Jack asked.

"It's a cheap bicycle," the mother said, fighting back her tears. "The kind no one would want to steal. A black color."

"It had a thick chain," the father added, "with a big brass lock, from China."

"A Chinese lock? A China brand?" Jack asked.

"Yes."

Jack gave them his card. "Call me if he telephones or comes back here," he said. "In the meantime, we'll take a look."

The couple began to offer profuse thanks.

Jack stopped them abruptly. "We can't *promise* anything," he said. " Maybe it's nothing, but stay by the phone in case we have to reach you." He looked at P.O. Wong who was already leaning toward the door. "You check out the Twelfth Street delivery," Jack said. "That's closer. Then meet me at the second drop if it's good."

They left the parents whose fearful looks followed them out, the mother wringing her hands.

Outside, Jack handed Wong a two-way radio. "I took it from the stationhouse," he said, "my cell is working so I'm good. But what's up with you? I thought you had the day shift."

"Nah," Wong answered, twisting the radio's volume dial to full blast. " I'm changing to nights. Was a discretionary thing."

"Yeah? How's that?"

"Between you and me, I didn't like working with the Sarge."

"Donahoe?"

"Yeah. Big 'Irish Don.' "

"What happened?"

"I overheard him talking to another sarge, saying how the Chinamen cops were no better than the *skirts.* "

Jack knew that meant female officers.

"He said we're short, and skinny," continued Wong, "and he

didn't feel he could depend on us in a chase, or a firefight."
Wong shook his head disdainfully, continuing, "This coming
from a guy who's almost three hundred pounds and couldn't
chase a wheelchair down the street without catching a cardiac."

"That's messed up."

"No doubt."

"Look, forget that stuff," Jack said, "You'll get with other
cops, *good* cop*s*, along the way."

"Yeah, right," Wong said cynically.

They split up at the corner, heading in different directions.
Jack, who had the longer trek, went toward the Riis Houses,
four long blocks east, then another four or five depending on
how the numbers ran. *Nine to ten blocks, a half mile, under the
falling snow, and into the river wind.*

Watch and Wait

Lucky glanced up at the night sky.

The snow was sticking, blanketing the streets beneath the
street lamps.

He'd met Skinny Chin coming out of the *see-gay* radio car
from LaGuardia, in front of Lee Watch on Orchard, and they'd
gone straight to his office safe. Skinny had pulled out the
shipping invoices for the watches and copied them on his
run-down China-made combo phone/fax/copier.

Lucky kept more than an arm's length from Skinny, watching him as he reached inside his jacket like he was pulling a gun, but he only came up with a lighter and a cigarette.

The copier chugged out some copies and Skinny handed them to Lucky.

"So you found the shit?" he asked bluntly.

What am I, a fuckin' detective? Lucky remembered thinking. "No," he answered coolly, "the boys noticed a few Fuk bitches wearing Movado and Rado. They wanted to be sure before snatching them."

"When did your *kei dai* punks ever need to be *sure* about anything they rip off?"

Lucky narrowed his eyes at him, saying, "There's a fuckin' truce on. You wanna start up some shit with the old men?"

"Hey, fuck that," groused Skinny. "Just let me know if you find anything."

Lucky nodded into Skinny's smoky exhalation, thinking how easy it would be to *wash* him, make him fuckin' disappear, if he didn't watch his words and his tone. As Skinny walked away, Lucky scanned the invoices, seeing several long columns of bar codes and serial numbers under the brand names. *What am I, a fuckin' detective?* he thought again, smirking.

He folded the papers and headed back to his condo. The black-faced Rado was in his safe, and he wondered if Koo Jai's number was about to come up.

Revelations

At his window six floors above the Bowery, Lucky held up the back of the black wrist watch to the light, looked for the last digits as he snubbed out the roach of Jamaican Gold into a teacup. He compared the digits to the ones on Skinny's list, blowing reefer fumes as he found what he was looking for.

He took a breath, checking the watch a second time for the full run of numbers, and matched up the eight digits. No doubt.

Fuckin' scumbag, thought Lucky, but grudgingly he had to give the kid credit: he'd underestimated him. *Showed balls, motivation, making money out there in no-man's-land, banging around against the Fukienese hard boys whose dialect they couldn't even understand.*

The matching digits also showed what a sneaky, daring motherfucker Koo Jai really was, pulling the rip-offs and keeping the swag.

Fuck the dailo, *right?*

Four guys pulling jobs? Why not? If they'd planned it right, in and out quick. Blame it on the Fuks anyway.

Watch your back. He heard the thought crashing forward from the back of his brain. *Play it off. Come down with fire on Koo Jai now and the Ghosts could lose East Broadway altogether. Play it cool and he'd get his piece, keep it all for himself this time, save the payback for later.* The rasta pot had mellowed him and from the haze he saw how he was going to deal with Pretty Boy cool Koo Jai. He'd gas him that he'd showed chutzpah, but that his crew still had to come up with twenty gees, because that piece was due the senior crews. Then everything would be settled, brothers again.

Oh, by the way, that includes the thousand I paid to your bookie. See how I'm covering your ass?

Deliver U$ from Evil

The falling flakes had made it all seem dreamlike. He tugged down his hoodie as he rode.

The first delivery was easy, thought Hong, practically around the corner from the takeout. A pretty blonde girl in a red sweater was waiting inside the street door of Number 129 when he rode up. She came out, gave him thirty dollars, told him "Keep the change and Merry Christmas" as he passed her the steaming plastic bag.

He never even got off the bike.

Looking east, he blew some snowflakes off his lips, and put his head down into the wind, his teenage heart shining inside with thoughts of Christmas, full of love glowing like a neon sign in the night. It wasn't like the city was shut down, he thought. Messy was more like it. He rode the beat-up bike through the slush, through the ruts and furrows in the snow plowed by people's feet stepping quick to get home for Christmas Eve. The ride was a slog, bumpy, but there were few people on the streets and he felt he was making good time, even with the flurries flying in his face.

He glanced back at the bags of food, still secured on the rear carrier, then took a few quick deep breaths, exhaling bursts of steam.

He dug his China-made knock-off Timberlands into the pedals, pushing and leaning forward, rolling toward the soft lights and shadows of the projects in the distance. As he rode, he felt the quiet anxiety that lurked in the back of his brain, concern for his own safety. But at least the rickety bike was holding its own. He remembered past trips there when neighborhood kids accosted him as he pedaled away after a delivery, calling after him "Ching chong chinky chinky," and yelling kung fu screams. But he also remembered the nice fat black lady who gave him a five-dollar tip after he delivered a large shopping bag of takeout for a party she was hosting. He could not remember which projects building that was, except that it numbered in the four hundreds.

He calmed himself by remembering that in the holiday season, people tended to be more generous with their tips, especially on cold, snowy nights. He thought about meeting up with his high-school friends later, and gradually made the right turn onto the long dim stretch of Avenue D, into the forbidding shadows of the Jacob Riis projects.

He passed several buildings, rolling beneath the naked branches of the tall trees twenty and thirty feet high, a skeletal canopy of limbs waving in the air above the lampposts, whipping shadows everywhere in the courtyard. He passed a raised platform of playground apparatus, realized that what he'd imagined were bodies huddled together were actually piles of black garbage bags somebody had hoisted there. A few more quick breaths.

On a hunch, he turned left, into a smaller courtyard hemmed-in by the high-rises, straining his eyes in the dim light looking for the numbers on the buildings. Following the curving line of lampposts that brought him around to brighter yellow glare, he began to decipher the numbers.

Great, he thought, having arrived at the first 400 building. He was proud that he'd come so close to the delivery address, his first try.

He chained the bike to the low iron railing that bordered the

playground area, double-checking the address on the receipt. He undid
the takeout from the rear carrier, and went across to Number 444.

When he entered the lobby he heard Christmas music playing some-
where, drifting down through the elevator shaft, carried along with the
faint smell of urine and feces. He tapped the elevator button, measured
his breathing, and considered having to make change for the customer.

The elevator door opened with a sound of scraping metal. He
instinctively peeped inside, making sure it was empty before stepping
in with the bags of food, knuckling the button for the fourteenth floor.

The floor numbers lit up as he was carried aloft, floating on the
Christmas music, thinking about the Chinese Club party, and how late
he was going to be . . .

On This Holy Night

The windy blasts from the East River had pummeled Jack
every breath of the four long and dark blocks through the
Alphabets—Avenues A, B, C, D—the frigid gusts shrieking
and driving the flurries sideways.

Avenue A was deserted except for a few lonely neon lights
in scattered storefronts.

He went past open lots, and areas set off by wire fences, filled
with debris, car parts, garbage, all partly frosted by the snow.

Avenue B began with derelict buildings. A bus pulled away in
the distance, too much of a sprint for him even in good weather.
He crossed over, walking along the tracks of the bus tires, until
he was able to cut across the park at Tompkins Square.

Walking from Avenue C to D, the wind tore at him with icy claws. His fingers got numb, and when he touched his Colt, he felt the frozen metal burn. He took quick breaths and blew on his hands. Almost to the corner, he could see the Riis Houses stretching outward above him. Some bunker-shaped buildings were only six stories tall, others beyond looked like fifteen flights or more. From what he remembered of his precinct review, the Riis consisted of nineteen red-brick towers lining Avenue D, built after World War Two, in part, to provide jobs and homes for returning war veterans.

The Riis Projects were once the most infamous of low-rent communities. Thirteen thousand apartments, currently still a significant source of the crimes that challenged the 0-Nine, still one of the meanest neighborhoods in the country.

He tapped the number on the delivery receipt into his cell phone. It went to voicemail again and he hung up. *Miller, Das . . .*

The building numbers ran down, south along the avenue. He was in the thousands and he figured another five blocks, somewhere around East Fifth then, leading him back toward the stationhouse.

The lighting was unnatural, especially where the yellow of the street lamps arcing overhead ran up against the black night sky. Nothing was clear, everything appeared in a flat monochrome, and his imagination created things that weren't there. The streets ahead were all shadows and the skeletal overhang of trees. To his left, he saw the backboards of basketball courts, and in the middle view beyond, the overpasses of the FDR Drive pointing to Brooklyn far in the distance. To his right, a run of bodegas, fried-chicken joints, a deli—all closed now behind the blinding veil of snow, and everywhere, covering everything, the dim yellow wash of the chromium light.

He didn't want to take it lightly, *missing* persons being what it was, but he also wanted to keep an open mind. Until proven otherwise. Trying to be objective, to keep his emotions out of it. It was mostly the mother's fears that drove the situation, but he felt the father wasn't sure. *Scared, but unsure. It wouldn't be the first time a high-school kid, a teenager, did something he shouldn't have.*

He marched forward, following the building numbers down.

Somewhere around Fourth Street, the last building, the address came up. He went toward the courtyard, wondering if P.O. Wong had found anything. *Probably the kid's back at the take-out already . . .*

Twenty yards in, he could make out the shape of a bicycle next to a railing, and getting closer, the building, Number 444. He decided to check the bike before trying the phone again. In the yellow light he saw where the heavy chain had obliterated the manufacturer's logo, a beat-down bike, cheap, its skin a scarred generic black. Some sort of modified carrier over the back tire. The bike leaned against the railing, held there by a big lock. When he brushed the snow off and rubbed away the tarnish, he could see that the clunky lock bore a Chinese character *sing*, for star.

He quickly scanned the courtyard grounds but saw not a soul. Fresh falling snow covered all tracks. He dialed the Miller number again, got voice mail again, and hung up. *Still, could be anybody's bike,* he told himself as he went toward the building.

Inside the lobby it was warm. He was glad to be out of the snow and wind. He stopped to catch his breath, but the air was foul. He heard Nat King Cole crooning a Christmas song through the PA system, and he tapped the elevator button, hoping the smell in there wouldn't be worse. The door scraped open. The smell was more garbage than human waste, and he tapped the button for Fourteen, measuring his breath through his mouth, Nat King Cole fading below him. He unzipped his jacket. Thinning his breaths past six, nine, to fourteen.

The door screeched open. A loud raucous hip-hop beat filled the long corridor, some rapper he didn't know, angry and cussin' about *nigga dis, an nigga dat. . . .* Fourteen D was left? Right? He followed the beat, a,b,c,d, into the corner, the strong smell of reefer bringing him around the bend.

The smell concentrated around 14D, though he couldn't be sure it wasn't seeping from one of the adjacent apartments, or if someone had puffed some quick hits in the dead end. He knocked on the door firmly, three times. When he heard the hip-hop turn down a notch he said, "Police, need to ask about . . ."

"Who?"

"Police. You had a food delivery recently . . ."

"Delivery? Nah, man, dat was uh hour ago."

"Could you open up, please?" Jack brushed his jacket back, cleared the draw to his holster.

"Yo!" the voice barked. *"Chop suey,* we busy up in here! STEP THE FUCK OFF!" The hip-hop beat boomed back up.

That did it for Jack. "Open the door!" he yelled. "Police!" He pounded on it, pulled out his Colt, and brought it up as the door opened.

"Don't understand English, muthafucka?" The man's jaw dropped when he saw Jack's gun. "Yo, chill," he said with red *ganja* eyes. "Yo, chill, chill, yo, chill, yo." His friend in the red do-rag brought his hands up above his head as Jack backed him into the dark apartment, the rap beat booming out into the corridor's dead end.

Jack couldn't see a wall switch. He yelled, "Turn the lights on!" a split second before he saw a brown flash, a pit bull lunging into the air at him. He twisted his body, folding himself down. A *praying mantis.*

The man in the red do-rag grabbed a baseball bat and swung as Jack dropped, pegging a shot even as he felt the dog's jaws clamp down on his left forearm, the frenzied pit bull's jerking, snarling head drooling blood and spittle.

Screaming, Jack jammed the Colt's barrel into the mad dog's ear and fired, splattering brain matter and blood as the animal suddenly went slack, its eyes still open. Jack rolled, his chest heaving, his heart hammering. He heard things smashing, then saw the bat come around a second time, splintering the wood table. He squeezed off two rounds, one of the bullets going through the bottom of the table. The man was falling backward. There was a big crash and then the screaming hip-hop stopped.

Jack shoved the dead dog's body away. With his left arm hanging, mangled and dripping blood, he started to push himself up, edging against the wall in a crouch. Suddenly, another shape, firing wildly, like firecrackers on Chinese New Year, ran toward the open door.

Shooting from the hip Jack answered with shots of his own, saw the blur of a black face under a white do-rag flinch before continuing out of the apartment. Following the sound of footsteps retreating, Jack heard his Colt's hammer snapping down on spent shell casings, his trigger finger jerking reflexively.

He flipped the barrel open and shook out the spent shells, tried for his reloader clip but his left arm only trembled. He tucked the barrel of the Colt under his left armpit and used his right hand to get the reloader from his jacket pocket. His left side shook uncontrollably as he reloaded, meanwhile thinking, *Pull the cell phone, turn the lights on, call for help.*

Footsteps and noise from the outside corridor.

The man in the white do-rag reappeared in the doorway as Jack slipped his finger over the Colt's blood-slicked trigger, ready to pull.

Then he heard the police radio, and suddenly the lights were switched on as P.O. Wong stepped out from behind the gangsta. Jack could see that the man was cuffed, and bleeding from the left leg. The wail of sirens came from the streets below, response to P.O Wong's 10-13, *officer down*, crackling over the radio.

"Caught him limping away from the building," Wong said. "Had this little shit gun on him. Called it in."

In the stark light Jack saw traces of blood everywhere. The first man had a sucking chest wound, bloody fingers caressing a big fake diamond cross on a chain, his eyes with a faraway look. A baseball bat lay near the dead pit bull who was staring at them with open jaws. And more blood, smaller scattered splatters, led toward the inside rooms. Blood that Jack didn't think was his, or theirs.

"Officer-involved shooting," Wong was barking into his radio. Then more sirens, distant, sounded below them.

Further inside stood a roach-infested kitchen table bearing empty containers of Chinese food, spilled cleanser, and plastic bottles of Windex, and Clorox, next to a thin roll of paper towels. *Someone's messy attempt to clean up.*

Jack stagger-stepped over to the take-out containers, saw a crumpled receipt. He unfolded it, and matched it to the copy he had in his pocket.

"Where's the kid? Where's the kid?" Jack yelled, feeling a sudden pinching pain in the left side of his chest.

"Don't know nuthin 'bout no kid!"

Jack took in a slow *tai chi* breath, exhaled, and said, "You're going down hard for this, punkass. You know that."

"Fuck you, man. I ain't done shit."

"Not yet. But you're going to do *life*, sucka—"

"Fuck you."

Keeping his eyes lowered, Jack fought the spasm of pain and the urge to pistol-whip the scumbag.

"Fuck you," again, as P.O. Wong pulled Jack away. "Fuck both yo *chinky* asses."

Jack propped himself against the wall. He was becoming lightheaded, his *chi*—energy—bleeding out of him.

The EMS rushed in. The techs took him, the cop, first, cutting up his left sleeve, pulling out loaded spikes for tetanus, painkiller. Combat meds and swabs.

"Fuck, *ma* leg's bleeding, too!"

"They'll get to you," Wong said, sitting him down opposite the man with the chest wound.

"Whoa," one of the techs said. "He's got a chest wound, too." They spread open Jack's jacket, cut open his shirt, found the wound. They checked his back, applied a compress.

146

"Surface," said one of the techs, as they patched him, laying him on a gurney, injecting him with another spike as they rolled him toward Wong, who was saying into the radio, "Major Case advised, *en route.* Request assistance to search for *missing person.*"

Other uniforms rushed in now.

"Find the kid," Jack said, grabbing Wong's arm. "Call the parents."

Then he was bumping into the stinking elevator as another EMS team arrived. Sliding through the courtyard, the cold fresh air rushing around him, into the ambulance under the yellow glow and blur of street lamps.

Then the night colors were flying by.

"Cabrini . . . Emergency," the EMS barked over the radio.

Just as the painkiller took hold he imagined a ringtone somewhere, familiar but distant. By the time he realized it was *his* cell phone, in his jacket somewhere, the gurney was rocking and swirling. He wondered if it was Alex calling, or Wong, or the parents of Hong, at the takeout, but then the medication swept over him, blotting out the light in his head, and tossing him into blackness.

Break
Down

Shorty pissed out the beer into the stained bowl of the closet bathroom, listening to Koo Jai angrily pacing the length of the long flat, grumbling as he went, tossing magazines, beer cans, and leftover takeout into the big plastic bag he dragged behind him. Shorty flushed the toilet, then swung open the small vent window. He could see that the street was dead quiet. For an instant, he recalled squeezing in through that opening, back when the flat served as the Stars hangout, and they had locked themselves out. He sure was the hero *that* day.

"You fucked up," bitched Koo Jai.

Emerging from the bathroom, Shorty wagged his middle finger at Koo Jai's back, saying "What the fuck . . ." almost to himself. He noticed the section of floorboard askew beneath the mirror, where Koo Jai hadn't kicked it back into place properly. The Stars used to store weapons there, and now, he figured Koo Jai was stashing swag as well. *The watches maybe, or some cash.* He thought of his last Movado, having sold the others and the Rolex as well. *The Stars had used another stash spot, by the front window.*

"You fucked up," Koo Jai repeated. "You jerked me off."

Shorty, tired of his complaining, said, "What the fuck didja want me to do? Tell the *dailo* no? He snatches me off the street, tells me to bring him up here. He's got that big gorilla with him, and I'm gonna argue?"

"You coulda called me first, jerk-off." Koo Jai steamed. "You coulda told him you could get hold of me by phone. You coulda gave me a heads-up."

"The boss said, 'Take me up there.'"

"*Call.* At least I wouldn't be standing there in my fuckin' underwear."

"The man said, 'Take me up.' So fuck you—"

"And fuck you, too," Koo Jai spat out. "Bitch."

"—*And* your fuckin' underwear." Shorty ran out, slamming the door.

"You fuckin' idiot!" screamed Koo Jai. Curses followed Shorty down the stairs.

"Asshole," fumed Shorty. *I'm the one opening the doors, and I can't get no respect? Fuck his pretty-boy faggot ass. Payback is a mean bitch.*

Back in the flat, Koo Jai tossed the full plastic bag at the door, anger boiling over, more unsettled now by the flow of events. *Dailo comes out here, gives us smokes and pills, tells us to watch the buses? He mentions the rip-offs. Are we being included, finally, with the inside crews? Or is somebody playing us along?*

Ghost Face

Lucky's thoughts shifted back to Koo Jai, and the twenty gees the wayward little dog would need to come up with.

His dragon's anger vented, Lucky's cool-down demeanor was restored. He saw the situation with new objectivity. He knew he could hide the hatred he still held inside, knew he could run his concerned-big-brother routine. He'd demand his take, insinuating there would be deadly consequences for failing to produce the cash out. But he'd go easy, give him some time to put it together. Wait until the cash got squared, until after the holidays, when things quieted down, before *chaat sai keuih,* erasing, the whole crew.

And he'd blame it on the Fuks.

That would put the old men on the spot. Then he'd lay back and see which dogs ran to which side.

He caught up with Koo Jai at the One-Six-Eight, sitting alone at the far end of the bar, chugging down a Tsingtao. Koo Jai was engrossed in some action flick playing on the television above the cash register and never noticed Lucky until he was behind him, the *dailo* grinning at him in the bar mirror. Koo Jai started to turn but Lucky put a hand on his shoulder, saying with a steely smile, "Just listen up."

Koo Jai noticed how the *dailo*'s gun hand never left his jacket pocket, which he held lifted slightly off his hip, a hard angle protruding. Again the steely grin. He knew Lucky could nail him before he'd make it off the bar stool.

"You got *hoots pa*," Lucky said, "Know what that means?"

Koo Jai shook his head uncertainly.

"It's Jewish," Lucky smirked. "Means you got balls."

The hand on his shoulder felt more reassuring now to Koo Jai.

"And that's a good thing," Lucky continued. "Smart, too, the way you've pulled it off."

Koo Jai smiled, dumbfounded.

Lucky's voice softened, saying, "We could use more guys with smarts and balls." *Playing him.* "But here's the problem. You still gotta square it up, what's due the senior crew, is due. Know what I'm saying?"

Koo Jai nodded his head like a bobble-head doll, mouth open, suddenly short of breath.

"Then everything would be even,"offered Lucky. "Brothers

all around, hah?" He paused. " Otherwise, too many people lose face." Another pause. "And you know, lose face and you lose lives."

Koo Jai felt like a fish, caught in a shrinking net.

"So, however you do it, I don't care. Call your crew together," Lucky instructed. "Dump the shit, whatever. Bring me twenty gees *cash*. I don't want any fuckin' watches, jewelry, no fuckin' bird's-nests. Nothing but cash. Twenty large, dollars." He could feel the wheels revving up in Koo Jai's head. "Look," the Big Brother said almost amicably, " I know it's Christmastime, and it ain't easy to cough it all up. I'll give you a coupla weeks, until the end of the year. How's that, huh?"

"Good," Koo Jai said meekly.

"Good. Because it's all about face. And the watches should be easy to move, with the holidays and gifts and all, right?"

Koo Jai smiled and nodded. Lucky patted him on the back, saying through an artifical smile, "And by the way, that twenty includes the gee I paid your bookie at the OTB." He watched Koo Jai's eyes go distant, then leaned closer, saying softly, "So merry fuckin' Christmas, *brother*."

And then he left him twisting on the stool at the run-down bar.

Fade In

Jack awoke to a bullet-gray sky pressed against the recovery-room window. He was unsure of where he was, and when he tried to change his position he felt tethered, tubes pulling at his arm, an IV drip above him, a blood packet hanging down.

And then Alexandra's clenched face breaking into a gentle smile.

"Easy, tough guy," she said.

"Where . . . ?" he began to ask.

"Cabrini Emergency." Alex brought her face closer. "It's nine-thirty AM."

"How long. . . ?" He coughed, trying to shake off the medication.

"I didn't see you at Midnight Mass so I figured something had come up. I called the precinct and found out you were here."

"What happened with the kid?" He rubbed his temple with his free hand.

"There was an Officer Wong at the nurse's station. He said he was following up."

"The parents . . . what happened?" He scanned the room for his clothes, didn't see them anywhere.

"Jack," Alex said quietly, " the doctor says you need to rest."

He closed his eyes, saw the yowling jaws of the pit bull, the flash fire from the muzzle of the Colt, the baseball bat arcing through the light.

"Yeah, rest," he said.

"There was a second call. Some other detectives involved—"

Major Case, he guessed, handling the shooting. He wondered where his gun was, figured Wong would've taken it per the officer-involved shooting rules, for tests. Forensics and Internal Affairs.

"But Jack, the doctor wants to keep you another night, for observation. You've got a chest wound, too."

Chest wound? Jack didn't understand, thought the meds had

affected his hearing. *A dog chewed my arm. What chest wound?* He brought his hand up over his heart, felt the layer of gauze and tape there.

Abruptly, the doctor, a haggard face and balding head in a white coat, poked his face past the vinyl curtain.

"Awake, great," he said, " Detective, how're you feeling?"

"Like crap," Jack answered, wondering about the pinching sensation in his chest.

"That's to be expected," the doctor said. "We're keeping you overnight, running rabies tests. And because of the chest wound, as a precaution."

Jack took a slow, deep, breath, felt something pulling in his left lung area.

The doctor continued, "Luckily, it was a through-and-through. Small caliber, in and out of your pectoral, just grazed the breastplate."

"Breathing feels tight," Jack said.

The doctor gave Alex a reassuring glance. "You're feeling the stitches," he said to Jack. "And you're lucky, Detective. If you'd had your torso twisted another inch that way, the bullet would have pierced your heart."

The punk-ass, firing wildly at him in the dark. He'd been hit and hadn't even realized it. He remembered instead the screaming pain of the dog's bite. He suddenly worried that the stitches in his chest would pop.

"So take it easy," the doctor continued, "Your commanding officer tells me it's the second time you've been wounded within three months."

Second time. He hadn't thought about the first shootout in Brooklyn, with the tall Chinese tong enforcer, Golo, who was in a Potter's Field now. He'd filed it away in the back of his mind, fallout from his tour in the Fifth Precinct.

The doctor looked for focus in Jack's eyes. "So," he continued, "I believe the department's got you scheduled for mandatory leave."

"Leave?" Jack asked, casting an unhappy look at Alex.

"Jack," she said, "it's for your own good. A procedural thing." She paused before adding "There's probably going to be a psych evaluation also. You'll be out for a while."

"Leave," Jack repeated softly to himself, his mind drifting. "It's Christmas Day," he suddenly remembered, looking at Alex, "and you're *here*."

"Well, Chloe's at my parents, until dinner. I was only going to SoHo, to shop a little. No biggie. Just wanted to make sure you were okay." She patted his hand.

There was a quiet moment, then the doctor said, "The nurse will be in shortly. You need to rest. And I'll look in on you in the afternoon."

"Thanks, Doc," Jack said, his mind still processing information. Then the phone rang somewhere close, *his* ring tone. Alex took his cell phone out of a closet in the side of the room. He caught a glimpse of his clothes inside as she handed it to him. He flipped the phone open, saw a number he didn't recognize, then heard P.O. Wong's tired voice.

"We found the body," he said.

God's General Gourd

She followed the wide ruts of truck tire tracks in the snow, turning the corner off Bayard.

In the Mulberry Street spirit shop, Bo checked the time, saw she still had an hour before her shift at the New Canton. She had wanted to pick up a tea, and a *bao*, a bun, along the way.

The shop smelled of jasmine and incense. There were bamboo umbrellas, ceramic gods and goddesses, lacquered dragons and Buddhas. She saw beaded bracelets, necklaces with Taoist trigrams, embroidered silk purses in all colors. As she searched, she remembered the words *cancer* and *radiation,* and wondered what talisman could ward off pain. Past a wall of cemetery items, candles and *death money,* there were strands of mini-temples and *bot gwa* talismans, amulets, and charm bracelets. She needed a different talisman. If *mercy* wasn't enough, she'd have to switch from the goddess Kuan Yin to a stronger, more masculine god. Naturally, she came upon Kwan Kung, General Kwan, *God of War.* Computer-etched onto the gold-plated metal card, Kwan Kung with his flowing black beard, his battle ax, and his fierce scowl was the one.

There was, after all, a war going on in Sai Go's body.

Bo also noticed the display rack of Good Luck Jade. She chose a solitary gourd of translucent pale jade, about the size of a nickel, hanging off a long strand of red, lucky thread. The gourd of the Shaolin monks, who used it to trap evil inside.

She paid for the items, carefully placing Sai Go's prescription and note inside the bag. At the door, she hesitated, mouthing a silent prayer before stepping back into the cold gray Chinatown morning.

Betting Against Time

The streets were frozen and the wind chill slashed at his bones.

He'd come back from the gambling trip with a gaunt face. He'd eaten heartily at the buffet tables whenever he found his appetite, but still he'd lost seven pounds.

As a matter of habit, Sai Go drifted in the direction of the OTB, but caught himself on the Bowery and turned toward the old park on Mulberry, which he knew would be desolate this time of year.

The west end of the park was where the old men usually gathered, in the open court or under the tall trees that circled an open pavilion. The stone structure had a gabled slate roof with eaves supported by simple ionic columns and arches. The pavilion was accessed by a rise of a dozen steps to an open expanse of tiled floor.

Sai Go remembered taking bets there in his earlier years. Now the space was deserted except for an occasional encampment of the homeless. Fronting the pavilion was an open court, in the middle of which stood a tall flagpole that looked like a tall white cross. The American flag was at the top, then a Parks Department flag and a New York City flag at quartermast, all drooping and dangling against the cold windless sky. Under the flags was an arrangement of tables and benches under the bare maples and walnuts, trees that were scarred not only by the extremes of the seasons, but by hacks and gouges from the knives and tools of the men who gathered there in good weather to play Chinese chess and checkers. Sometimes crowds three-deep surrounded a good match, all men, smoking cigarettes and swapping tales and memories.

Memories.

He was drawing on memories now, reviewing parts of the life that had brought him to this end. Sitting alone, on the bench under the naked trees, he clutched the Buddhist mercy talisman, and contemplated the rest of his dying days.

Blanket Party . . .

Wong had worked along with the two extra uniforms who'd stayed behind, canvassing in the darkness, checking the adjacent buildings.

They searched the maintenance areas: a New York City Housing Authority gardener's shed, and a fenced-in lot for dumpsters and garbage bins. They checked the cages where the porters and mechanics stored supplies, and the loading docks where they staged the project's garbage for pickup.

Nothing.

Just the cops freezing their asses off on Christmas morning, slogging through the graveyard run.

The man with the wounded leg had clammed up. EMS had taken him to Beth Israel Emergency, together with his homeboy with the hole in his chest.

Wong continued diligently through the night, the falling

snow covering everything, wiping out any track or trail. Toward dawn he was advised via radio that a senior detective would be assisting. Pasini, something. *Use to be senior dick in the 0-Nine until he transferred to Staten Island.*

Daylight came as they were searching rooftops.

Some projects children, playing in the drifts in FDR Park, noticed the pretty *red* snow, the crimson liquid seeping out of an icy mound. Buried beneath was a bulky shape inside black garbage bags. A parent notified one of the uniforms on the incoming shift, who then radioed P.O. Wong.

"Near the crossover—the overpass—park side, about Sixth Street."

Inside the black bags, they found a battered body, loosely wrapped in an Oakland Raiders bedsheet and a ratty comforter. At first, Wong couldn't tell the victim was Chinese, the head and face were so beaten, beyond recognition, a pulpy mass red with blood. Black hair matted down, a corpse wearing a gray jacket stained red-black, with a hoodie attached, Timberland boots on his feet.

His blood had found its way out of the wrapping, gravity working to stain the white flakes like a cherry snow cone.

Wong was shaken and fatigued, but knew he'd have to manage in the following hours, and days.

As the ME's wagon carried the body away, he noted on his report *Notify parents, positively identify body,* knowing whoever was going to pick up the case would need all the information about the two gangsta perps.

In the cold naked daylight he went back to the takeout where he found the parents still waiting behind the shuttered gates, almost hysterical, fearful of the worst. Upon seeing Wong, the mother began to cry. The father put his arm around her shoulders, and Wong said to him, "We think we've found him."

"Think?" The father took halting breaths.

"We need you to come, to identify the . . . to make sure . . ." Wong struggled, as both parents wailed and collapsed against each other.

Above and Beyond

Jack dressed quietly, letting the nurses pass on their rounds.

He knew neither perp was going anywhere. He called in a trace of the telephone number used to place the take-out orders and went straight from the Discharge Unit to the crime scene at Four-Forty-Four, walking through the slush. The rear of the projects was just as ugly in daylight. He went past the word NIGGAZ in big block letters proudly tagged in black marker across the building's cinderblock wall. It didn't strike him as a *power* word, not professing ownership of anything but self-hatred. He felt the *word* was just niggers with a different shine on it. It was *a black thing,* he'd been told; *you* wouldn't understand.

He found the super, went past the Crime Scene tape into 14D.

Stepping carefully through the scene, he remembered the progression of events like a series of snapshots: red do-rag fronting him, the screaming hip-hop music, the pit bull coming out of nowhere. Flashes of gunfire, the racking pain, then the wild gunfight. He'd emptied his Colt. Looking back, he realized he'd been fighting off shock, trying to stay focused in those moments, blood draining from him even then.

Everything else had been just background.

Now, it was *all* background, Crime Scene Unit having been all over it, anything important to the investigation already carted away. Seeing it in daylight now, a stack of dirty plastic dishes in the sink, a half-empty sack of dog food, crushed take-out containers scattered across the floor, cockroaches all over.

Jack knew this run-down projects apartment was typical, a haven for junkie absentee parents and illegitimate drop-out children, siblings, and cousins mixed in together in an environment of violence and drugs.

In the bedroom, piles of dirty clothing lay on top of bare mattresses. There was a scatter of broken and stained furniture, a couple of filthy sleeping bags in the corners, jackets and boots against the wall. The place was more like a homeless encampment than a residential unit. There was a stack of fuck magazines on top of a dresser. *Ghetto Bitches, BadAss Hos, Black Pussy Mamas,* black girls fondling and spreading themselves for the camera. Next to the stack, a crumpled photograph of the two *killas* and a third youth, making gang signs, posing somewhere in one of the project's courtyards. The one he'd shot in the chest had his hair done up in fifty-dollar cornrows, long enough to trail stiffly off the back of his neck, smiling out a mouth of gold caps, flashing CZ studs in both ears.

The one he'd shot in the leg wore a New York Knicks cap, and an Oakland Raiders football shirt. A thick silver chain with a big cross of shiny glass chips dangled from his neck. Putting on a hard thug look for the camera.

The third youth wore a black T-shirt tucked into a big silver belt buckle encrusted with glittery letters that spelled out the word ICE, his baggy jeans threatening to slide off his hips. Challenging the camera with his gangsta sneer.

All three living large. Posing and fronting.

He pocketed the photo.

Jack noticed a foul odor coming from the bathroom. He saw an empty jug of Lysol there. From the grimy kitchen window, he could see the four lanes of the FDR Drive below, running north-south, and the overpass that spanned them, the ramp next to where they'd found the body. *A high-school scholar, dumped in cold blood like a sack of garbage by the gutter. Sai m'sai,* what a waste.

Looking across the East River to the Brooklyn waterfront, to Williamsburg, he saw dilapidated docks and crumbling warehouses along the piers, camouflaged by the clean cover of snow. Garages and gritty industrial dumpsites along a graffiti-tagged and run-down shoreline. An area slowly being converted to residential lofts and low-rise condos, with pioneering urban homesteaders paving the way for the gentrification that was sure to come, the reality of realty finding its way across the river from Manhattan.

His focus came back to the apartment. *A rag in the kitchen corner. Streaks of blood along the baseboard.* There was a cracked-open boom box lying on its side. He squatted down, tapped the play button. The box exploded into a hip-hop rant, angry yelling rapping blasting the small space, a homemade recording, that sounded like:

Whup dat Chinee
Whup dat Chinee

161

Beat him down,
Down wit da hamma,
Beat him down!

Thump dat yellow
Eveebody hello!
Slam wit da baseball
Bat dat Chinee
Bat dat Chinee
Mutha-Fucka!

Stab the blade down
Punch it up
Whup da Chinee
Chop chop chop
Thump dat yellow
Slam dat Chinee
Mutha-Fuck!

Which then faded to a chorus of

Huh huh
Yo! Yo!

Stunned by the lyrics, Jack hit the Stop button, and wondered if Crime Scene had bothered to play it.

Killing chinks was fun now.

Call it a blanket party. *Yo! Yo!*

A dull throbbing pain moved down his left side. *The meds wearing off.*

He pocketed the tape.

His cell phone buzzed; they had an address. Five-Twenty-Six. Apartment 4C. One of the corner buildings.

He left the crime scene, the icy wind dulling the pinching pain in his left chest. He took one of the uniforms with him, a veteran black officer who'd worked the regular vertical patrol before Housing and Transit were merged into one NYPD. A Community Affairs officer.

Jack showed him the photo. "Looking for this kid, *Ice*," he said.

The cop shook his head sadly. "Tyrone. Lives with his grandma." He broke down the kid's story.

Tyrone Walker, eighteen, was a punk-ass wannabe, wanting to be in with the Eastside Blunts, wear the colors. A *fronting* punk-ass coward. Even the Blunts could see that, playing him along, but not blooding him in, using him as a go-fer.

Now he'd brought cop heat to the drug projects and the projects had given him up.

Together, they dragged him out of his grandma's apartment closet in Five-Twenty-Six, cowering in fear. They tossed him in a cab, cuffed and whimpering. When they got to the 0-Nine Jack took a Polaroid of Tyrone before putting him in a holding cell.

Down the hall, the other perp sat cuffed to a table inside the interview room the cops had nicknamed "the cooler." He was *chillin' like a villain.*

According to the notes an exhausted P.O. Wong had left on Jack's desk, the shooter in the cooler was DaShawn Miller, eighteen, with a rap sheet that detailed his ascent of the thug ladder: early busts for loitering, drinking from an open container, turnstile-hopping, then from criminal mischief to purse-snatching, to menacing, assault, possession of controlled substances, possession with intent to sell, and now finally, gun possession and attempted murder of a New York City police officer. The investigation would be ongoing.

The other perp, the one with the bat, who Jack had shot in the chest, was Jamal Bryant, or JB, aka *Jelly Bean,* also eighteen, with a juvie file that had been sealed by the court, which meant the kid had committed some heinous felony, that he was a damaged child, possibly a danger to others, a menace to society, but because of his age, the courts in their wisdom had decided he was to receive correction and rehabilitation. Following that, Jamal had had a few other beefs: shoplifting, burglary, auto theft.

Both had dropped out of Seward Park High, and fallen into the thug life.

Gangsta Rap

Detective Pete Pasini, who knew the precinct, knew the Riis Houses and the thug culture that bred there, was assisting the investigation through Major Case, fielding it during Jack's short disability. A thickset man, he had a grizzled pockmarked face, and looked more like a Mafiosi than Major Case cop.

Jamal Bryant, with tubes sticking out of him, had given the middle finger to Pasini's questions at Beth Israel Emergency, then immediately passed out. *Tough-guy villain,* Pasini had thought, leaving him with the nurse, guarded by the uniformed officer posted at his door. *Fuck him,* Pasini had thought, *I don't need him right now anyway.* It wasn't like he was going anywhere anytime soon.

DaShawn Miller's wound wasn't serious, not life-threatening, so they'd patched him up and the uniforms took him back down into the stationhouse.

Observing them in the cooler, from behind the mirror glass in the watch room, Jack saw Pasini hand DaShawn a cup of water. When he was done drinking they'd have his fingerprints on the cup, and his DNA inside. An old trick.

Pasini wore a sympathetic face, worked his act like a Father Confessor, the good cop.

Jack tried to place DaShawn's face, flashing past in his mad dash from the apartment. A pair of deep-set eyes, and a flat nose with thick greedy lips below. A face crossed with fatigue and anger.

Jack buttoned the speakers, saw Pasini look up toward the sound before taking the empty cup with him.

In the watch room Pasini said quietly, "You up for this?"

"All the way," Jack answered.

"Look, it's *your* case," said Pasini. "The chief just needs to know you're okay with it, the vic being Chinese and all."

"Not a problem."

"I didn't want to push him into lawyering up. But he's playing tough guy anyway."

They watched DaShawn yawn, then spit on the floor through gold-capped teeth.

"Let's see *how* tough," Jack said.

"Step in anytime you're ready."

Jack nodded, took a slow, deep breath, and felt the pull of the stitches in his chest. He stepped into the cooler and heel-slammed the door behind him.

Bitch Up and Turn

DaShawn looked up, disgusted, whining, "Aw, man. Not you again."

Jack had figured that DaShawn was weak.

Wordlessly, Jack placed a tape recorder on the table and activated it.

DaShawn sneered at the recorder. The machine started pounding out the gangsta rap lyrics of the tape taken from the crime scene. DaShawn was stunned to hear it so loud in the small room, surprised that the yellow cop had picked up on it.

Jack circled behind him, let the rap run a few more beats before stopping the machine. He stood to one side of DaShawn, saying into the sudden silence, *"Whup dat Chinee,* huh? *Chop, chop, chop?"*

A nervous grin tightened DaShawn's face.

"Funny, ha?" Jack said, leaning in, saying in a soft voice. "You *shot* me, you little bastard. Shoot a cop? That's attempted murder. That alone gets you twenty-five to life. Shit, you really hit the big time now, son." He took the tape from the recorder and waved it in front of DaShawn.

"That gives you motive. You're a hater," Jack said, slapping down the photograph of the three boyz in the hood. "That's

you and the gang." Using the evidence like a box cutter, slicing away at the would-be hard-ass.

DaShawn's eyes danced over the photo even as Jack flipped down the Polaroid shot of Tyrone. "And that's your homey, Tyrone." Jack paused before adding, "Who, by the way, says it was *you*. He says you killed the delivery boy."

"Boo-shit," protested DaShawn.

"Tell you what, homeboy," Jack sneered, "you're going down for this shit. We've got the Chinese kid's blood on the bat. And the hammer. And your prints are all over them."

"So whut?" DaShawn said. " Lotsa people prints there, yo. We all played baseball, so whut?"

"And on the hammer? You all played *hammer*-ball?"

"Yeah, we wuz fixing up the crib, doing the Home Depo . . ."

"Smart-ass huh? Well, your boy Jamal also says it was you all the way."

"Nah, he ain't said no shit like dat."

"Oh yeah, *you*, all the way. Gave you up to save his own sorry ass."

"Nah, nah, you trying to gas me, yo."

"Jamal said *you*, with the bat, swinging for the yard."

"Nah, playing me wit dis *boo*shit."

"Tyrone said *you*, with the hammer."

"Tryin' ta punk me . . ."

"Did you do the stabbing, too? Where's the knife?"

"I ain't stab no one."

"You're saying Jamal stabbed him?" Jack continued. "Or you *both* stabbed him? Or you *took turns* stabbing him?"

"Neither one of us! And Jamal ain't said nuthin like dat."

"You? Or Jamal? Or Tyrone?"

"Man, step offa dat shit."

Jack leaned down, put his palms on the table, disgust on his face, and said, "You're looking at *life*, son. This isn't TV here, you can't change the channel. Better tell the truth, because Jamal and Tyrone are offering up your dumb ass, said you had the gun, you led the way. You know what a life sentence is like?" Jack smiled, shook his head slowly. "No weed. No pussy. Matter of fact, you're going to *be* the pussy. Telling you, better fess up, son."

"*Boo*shit, all booshit."

"Jamal turned on you, kid. Bitched up and turned. He said he's not doing the bid for what *you* did. Tyrone, too. Said *you* bugged out. All he wanted was some Chinese food, but you got carried away."

"Lying, you lying."

"Plus we got you with the gun. That's A-One Attempted Murder. On a cop, too."

"We ain't know you wuz a cop. Chinee? Shit. You ain't had no uniform on. We thought you wuz coming back from the takeout, looking for a tip."

"You're lucky if you don't get the needle."

"Nah, man, I ain't know you wuz a cop."

"You *ain't know* I was a cop? I yelled it out, fool. In *English*, not *Chinee*."

"We ain't heard shit. Wu Tang was slammin' off the player, we couldn't hear shit. All we saw was *ching chong* in the peephole."

Jack huffed, " And you know what? The Big Surprise?" smiling a Chesire Cat smile. "We got your DNA, too. Wanna bet we match it on the kid's body?"

DaShawn slowly waggled his head in disbelief, speechless.

" Jamal said you needed money. He said—"

"No, he ain't. No, he ain't."

Jack straightened up, took a breath, and said, "Last chance. I'm tired. I want to go home and sleep. Take a nap. Who the fuck needs this?"

DaShawn was squeezing his fingers, rubbing his knuckles, the jittery bird in his eyes. *Tyrone? Punk-ass Tyrone? But not Jamal.*

"I'm tired," Jack repeated. "Maybe I'll just pass this shit along to the DA. If you don't want to deal to save your own ass? Fuck you then. It's a slam dunk anyway."

" Jamal?" DaShawn started drifting. " Nah, *boo*shit."

"You're all going down. It's just a matter of how long. I can hook you up now, or you can lawyer up. Whatever. Personally, I don't give a fuck."

He watched DaShawn's stare go distant.

"*Game*time, DaShawn." Jack went toward the door. "Fuck, just let the DA charge you. Murder is a bitch bid, kid." He chopped down the door latch.

A low rumble came out of DaShawn. The rumble sounded like *aah-ite* and built to a roar as he slammed his fists on the table.

"Aaahite!! He screamed. "Aaaahiite!!"

Jack put a fresh tape into the recorder.

"Tell it." He thrust the machine forward.

Takeout

"When the delivery came Jamal said, 'Run the cash, *ching chong.*' Then the Chinese kid went into his pocket and Jamal hit him in the back with the hammer. The kid threw the money

169

to the floor. He started yelling and crying, trying to git away. Then Tyrone stabbed him and Jamal tossed a blanket over him, still beating him with the hammer. Tyrone kept stabbing into the blanket 'cause he kept moving, kicking his legs. Then Jamal grabbed the bat and hit him real hard on top and he went down. Jamal, mo times wit da bat. The kid was still crying but not so loud anymore. Tyrone finished him off with the hammer, 'til he didn't move no more."

DaShawn took a breath, was quiet a long moment. "I thought we wuz jes gonna rob him," he said. "I know Jamal wanted money for sneakers, but I didn't know Tyrone and him wuz gonna kill the guy. Swear to God, yo."

Jack leaned back and caught the rest of DaShawn's version.

"After, Jamal got mad. He was bitchin like 'Damn. Chinee muthafucka only had fitty-one dollas.' Tyrone was laughing, saying, 'Shit, Nigga. No Air Jordons fo yo nigga ass!' Jamal started cursing 'Ah'ma have ta git two mo dese chinkees fo enough paper, yo.' Tyrone said 'So call in another takeout, nigga,' but Jamal slapped him, said, 'Everyone is closed now, fool.' Then he was yelling, 'Come on, clean dis shit up! Move dis ching-chong mofukka outta here before five-o comes down.' Tyrone saying 'Lookit all the blood. Red, too.' He thought Chinee blood was yellow. They was laughing."

Jack felt his hatred rise. They were all laughing, a hysterical joke, even as they wrapped the body, sponged up the blood. He stopped the tape recorder, made DaShawn scribble a statement implicating the other two.

"It was dem who done it. Tyrone and Jamal, they killd the Chinee kid."

Jack took the signed statement and the tape, left the room,

and went back to the detective's area. Pasini waited there, grinning like he was impressed.

Jack reloaded the rap tape, readied the photographs. He gave Pasini a nod and headed for the holding cell where Tyrone was waiting to turn on his pals.

The Medical Examiner's report had been delivered by one of the uniforms, who'd placed it in the wire basket on the detective's table. It had Pasini's name on it but Jack opened it anyway, took a long hard look.

Grisly morgue pictures of the teenager Hong's body. Seen at different angles the body had thirteen stab wounds, from a knife blade eight inches in length, front and back, torso, stomach, shoulder, back, and arms, *just everywhere*. Some of the thrusts pierced his stomach and exited out of his lower back.

One stab had pierced his heart.

Six additional wounds to the head and shoulders, round quarter-size indentations about a half-inch deep. Blunt force impressions. One of the gangstas had swung the hammer like he was doing demolition work.

Metacarpus, phalanges. Broken fingers, both hands. Defensive wounds.

Fractured ulna, left forearm. Warding off the blows.

Fractured tibia, fibula, right side. A broken leg, dislocated kneecap. Kicked and hit going down.

Separated clavicle, the shoulder.

Three broken ribs on the left side. *The bat.*

An evidence photo of a Paul O'Neill *Yankee Slugger,* autographed model.

Shattered discs at the base of the spine, and higher, at the back of the neck. The bat, a swinging, killing club. Hitting home runs against Hong's body flailing underneath the blanket.

The face has fourteen bones. In Hong's face, twelve of these had been shattered. Mandible, palate, malar: jawbone, mouth, cheek. The black wood cracking through bone and gristle and teeth, crashing through nose and mouth.

A mutilated, destroyed face, then another photo showing a heavy metal Estwing, the claw hammer ripping out the nasus, the nose, the cartilage of septum, also the left eyeball (found in blanket). Facial structure crushed. Shattered occipital orbits, with skull fragments driven into the temporal areas. Displaced mastoid, and on and on, each notation consistent with a ball bat or hammer blow to the face.

Jack didn't know if it was because of the side effects from the painkillers, but he felt sickened. He knew that this horror went on every day in this city, in America, in the world.

There were more than thirty incidences of blunt-force damage.

Jack took a breath, closed the report. In his head he was hearing grievous groaning and sobbing, the banshee wail welling up around the sad street of funeral parlors across from the playgrounds of his youth.

Death and Desperation

Koo Jai stepped away from Canal and went down Baxter, entering Chinatown the back way, through the park, and away from Mott Street where he'd risk running into Lefty. Or Kongo and the crazies crew. But he needed a sense of what was coming his way because he didn't have what the *dailo* demanded. *Fuck!* That fuckin' wristwatch and that stupid cunt were his downfall.

Coming around to Mulberry, in the distance, a funeral taking place. *Fuck!* He'd put together eight thousand, and of course the bunch of watches the *dailo* didn't want. *Fuck that,* he wasn't about to dump the Rolexes, Cartiers, and Rados, worth ten thousand at least, even if he was desperate. *Fuck that.* And none of the crew came up with any money, all full of excuses. They'd hoped to plead their case to the *dailo,* hoped that reason would prevail. *Fuck them, too.* He thought of Sai Go the bookie, whom he was now certain had complained to the *dailo.*

The funeral band started, warming up despite the cold day. Three brass trumpets and a trombone, and two drums, a snare and a bass. Pacing a slow walk to a sad dirge.

If he saw him at OTB, fuck Sai Go, too.

A few black-garbed relatives came outside to smoke cigarettes, the smell of incense billowing out behind them.

To avoid their bad karma following him, Koo Jai crossed away from the section of funeral parlors, and stayed to the park side, to where Worth led him around a bend to OTB, and later, back to East Broadway, anguishing, *Right, where the fuck am I getting twelve thousand?*

He thought momentarily of robbing the Fuk mahjong club but knew it would be heavily guarded during the holidays. fuckin' *hak,* bad luck, he cursed. *Black karma* was following him.

* * *

173

Outside the Wah Fook funeral parlor, the drivers maneuvered their black Lincoln Town Cars for the day's processions. Two trips in the morning, one in the afternoon. The Hong funeral, the smallest of the three, led off, a flower wagon trailing the dark hearse, ahead of four Lincolns and a minivan.

Earlier, the Fukien East Lions group had trekked down to the Alphabets and performed a lion dance in front of the New Chinatown takeout to drive away the evil spirits. One member set off a mat of firecrackers, the staccato blasts shooting forth bits of colored paper that settled on top of the frozen slush.

A squad car sat on the corner of Fifth Street, watching, but the uniforms refrained from citing the illegal fireworks ban.

At Alexandra's suggestion, the Chinese Health Clinic had dispatched a team of Chinese-language grief counselors to the Hong home, an illegal basement rental in Sunset Park. The parents, who hadn't slept in two days, were racked with grief, in stunned disbelief at their loss, their only son, their joy and their hope, the A-student who was going to *be* someone in *Mai quo* Fukienese America, gone, forever lost to brutal, senseless violence. Gone, their American dreams all gone. The murderers, *hok-kwee* black devils, teenagers too lazy or stupid to succeed in school, their brains dulled from drugs and alcohol, their hearts hardened by racism and hate, animal souls consumed by lust and violence.

The grief counselors were themselves stunned.

Sociopathic was a word not found in the Chinese language, an idea the parents could not comprehend. *How could human beings have no regard for the evil they do? Unless, of course, they weren't human beings but* m'hai yun, *a lower species of animal.*

What could the grief counselors say? None of it made any sense.

In China, a criminal who committed murder would have received a *Beijing haircut,* a single nine-millimeter bullet to the head, followed by government's bill to the executed person's family for the price of the bullet.

In China, Jack knew, cops were liberal in their application of the law, justice there more pragmatic: do the crime, and you were executed. Simple as that, in a country with a billion people. There was no death row. There was no twenty years of appeals. China was six thousand years of civilization. They knew what worked. And they didn't *play.*

He watched the funeral gathering from a distance, near the ball fields of his childhood.

The neighboring businesses on the street, from the undertaker at one end to the headstone cutter at the other, were all moved by the tragic death, and had contributed to the funeral, according to the Chinese press.

The Chin brothers' Kingdom Caskets Inc. donated the simple bronze-colored coffin, a no-frills metal-veneer box.

Peaceful Florist discounted the floral wreaths, and the family's village association paid for the funeral and the plot.

Several radio-car drivers had offered to drive the family for free to the cemetery in Brooklyn and back to Chinatown.

On the park side, a group of Buddhist monks from the Temple of Noble Truths concluded their prayer service and planted sticks of incense in the iron urn by the curb.

A group of Puerto Rican schoolgirls passed by and cracked jokes, goofing on the bald heads and saffron robes of the monks. *Chino Viejo! Oh snap, like kong foo,* their giggling cutting through the dirge.

Inside the Wah Fook parlor the air was thick, heavy with the pungent cloud of jasmine incense that cloaked the room. The overhead lights were dimmed to set off the glow of candles softly illuminating the gathering of grieving, sobbing faces.

A small gathering, barely twenty people.

Out by the main doorway, the reporters and photographers waited at a respectful distance. Jack walked by them and made his way to the incense urn, paying his respects by planting three sticks of incense and bowing. Stepping to the casket, he bowed again, turned, and came to offer condolences to the family before returning to the main door.

The reporters made notes in their pads, a sad end to another violent New York City story.

Another dead Chinese deliveryman.

There is enough anger here, Jack felt, *in this small room. But where was the greater rage out there in the community? Would the Fukienese demonstrate again? Or would the old-guard Chinatown Cantonese make a statement?*

No justice, no peace?

No just us, no please?

The community's activist media would stay focused on this, Jack thought, and the DA's office would be very aware of that. This one wasn't going to be bargained away in some sealed juvie deal.

There was a freestanding black-and-white photograph of Hong, a smiling teenage face, just above the altar space. Below that was the closed casket the parents were forced to accept, so horrified were they by the damage to their son's face.

A ring of flowers surrounded the closed coffin.

They could hear the band starting up across the street on the park side, a sad sweet "Nearer, My God, to Thee" in four-four time.

The pallbearers readying themselves to shoulder the load.

Suddenly, the mother uttered a harrowing cry, then exploded from her seat and threw herself across the coffin, knocking over her son's framed photograph. The father and relatives rushed over to console and to restrain her. The mother was screaming, *"Aah Jai! Ah Jai!!"* and beating her chest, trying to tear her heart out, clutching at her hair. She fell to the floor, kicking, pounding the polished stone with her fists.

The relatives lifted her up, managed to slump her onto a seat, surrounding her from all sides supporting her, all of them wailing now, words useless in the whirlwind of grief.

The father stood speechless, ready to collapse.

The pallbearers lifted the casket, slowly beginning to walk toward the street. The band urged them on, the hearse standing at the curb with its tailgate open.

Up and down the street, drivers waited patiently as the pallbearers stepped slowly through the frozen morning, loading the coffin into the vehicle. The mother collapsed again and they carried her into one of the Town Cars. The band played until the last car moved off around the bend to Bayard, en route to the New Chinatown, then to Brooklyn, and on to everlasting sorrow.

HENRY CHANG

Life Is Suffering

Sai Go sat in the barber chair and watched Bo in the mirror wall of the New Canton. She caught his glance and raised the chair, pumping the lever with her foot to position him.

"You look tanned," she said with a smile. *And tired,* she thought. "Had a good time?"

"Yes," answered Sai Go as she draped the plastic sheet over him, discreetly returning the clinic card and prescription note. "You left them here last time," she said, grabbing a spray bottle.

Sai Go recognized the items immediately and nonchalantly pocketed them.

"Thanks," he said. "And I've got something for you, too." He produced a souvenir key ring with the Disney World logo, pleased by the happiness it brought to her face when he handed it to her.

"It's got a light." He smiled. "When you press the button. For the dark places."

"A wonderful gift." She beamed, flashing the light. "Thank you much." She remembered the talismans she had for him, but decided to wait until the end of the massage before showing them to him.

She misted his hair.

"The weather was good," Sai Go said. "We went all over."

Bo worked the little electric clipper against the long black comb.

"People swimming. People having fun," he continued.

She misted again, and he squinted at the comb whipping

178

around, chased by the buzz of the blades, hard salt-and-pepper clippings spraying across the plastic sheet.

"Everyone out in the sun," he said, blinking.

"Just like a postcard," Bo said, focused on the top of his head.

Sai Go felt himself floating, drifting behind his eyes. He scanned the overcast street in the mirrors, and felt detached, out of place. When he brought his focus back, he saw his quick trim, neat and tight. Bo was dusting his neck with powder, brushing him off. She loosened the plastic sheet.

He closed his eyes as Bo's strong fingers kneaded the knots where the cords ran from his neck into his shoulders. He took a slow deep breath, released it the same way. He thought he'd felt something catching in his chest as she massaged his shoulders.

Inside his forehead he imagined palm trees and blue skies, the hot Florida sun on his face. Her thumbs dug into the base of his skull, rotated there, and then her forearms pressed and rubbed the sides of his neck.

He imagined a pack of greyhounds sprinting around a track, chasing a mechanical rabbit, and remembered he'd fallen asleep during the last race, but still came out a winner, a grand fifty dollars on the day.

Gum Sook's herbal tea had made him feel good the first two days, then his energy faded and he became tired. He was sleepless the last days of the trip.

"When you get back, go to Sister Kee the herbalist," recommended Gum Sook. "Put together litchi and seaweed. Boil garlic and chives with duck eggs. Mix in red wine and royal jelly. Eat and drink like a thick soup. For two days. I'll write it down so she'll know what to do."

He'd appeared weak, and the two da jops, kitchen helpers,

made sure he got home okay after they'd landed at LaGuardia. A *see gay,* radio car, returned them to Chinatown, and he'd slept most of the first day back. He woke up remembering his regular massage and haircut appointment, and the key ring.

Bo felt Sai Go sagging, drifting, with his eyes shut, to another place. She was sad to see how drained he looked, sensing that he was slowly dying. She chanted a Buddhist prayer in her head that never showed on her face as she drove her elbows into the clenched muscle behind his lungs, pushing the cancers back.

Sai Go opened his eyes as he started to nod off, jerking his head backward. Bo gave him a final squeeze and began drumming his back with her fists. When she was done, she presented him with the talisman Kwan Kung card and the jade gourd, slipping the red cord of the pendant over his head.

Sai Go was touched, not only by her healing hands, but by her generous compassion, which he didn't understand, and didn't feel he had the time to figure out. Here was a woman, working hard and saving every dollar to pay off the snakeheads so they wouldn't turn her into a whore, and yet she presented him with new talismans, trinkets he'd seen for sale on Chinatown streets that had probably set her back twenty dollars. Cheap enough, but it was the thought, he reminded himself.

"Thank you," he said meekly. "But you shouldn't have," aware of the precariousness of her financial situation. He gave her the usual tip, but when he tried to pass her an extra twenty, she became *hock hee,* indignant, about accepting payment from him.

It was not Sai Go's style to force it upon her.

"It's only a small gift," she said firmly. "Why won't you let me enjoy giving something to you?"

He had nothing to say to that.

"How about this," he suggested. "I'll bet the twenty on a horse for you. It'll be like Lotto, okay?"

Offered a chance to test her luck, she couldn't refuse. A small smile broke through and she said, "If you like."

"Good then," he said, relieved. "I'll bring you the ticket."

At the OTB, Sai Go reviewed the list of entries and settled on the eighth horse in the eighth race, an eight-to-one underdog. Sai Go watched the odds changing across the board, the smart money running to the number five and number two horses, driving their odds down. The number eight horse looked even better to him then.

The teller at the window was confused when he saw the resident bookie purchase a legitimate ticket. He noticed Sai Go's sickly pallor and thought better of making a wisecrack.

Sai Go paid quickly and avoided any players who were looking for action. On the street he bought a small silk jewelry purse. It cost a dollar and he chose a red one for luck, red with gold embroidery. He tucked the OTB ticket inside and zipped it up.

He returned to the New Canton and gave it to Bo, saying, "Look for the race on the *deen see*, TV, or check the papers. You have the number eight horse, named *American Freedom*. I hope it's lucky for you."

Bo ran her fingers over the red silk, holding the purse as if it was precious, and said, "Thank you," so softly it seemed she was whispering to herself. She watched him go back out into the street, slowly crossing in the direction of Chatham Square, a tanned face against a dingy gray background of storefronts.

At the far corner, he paused and glanced back, and for an instant she believed she saw a smile on his face.

Space for Time

The world below was a cloudy gray drift of mountain ranges and valleys with the occasional appearance of roads, a small city or village. He'd passed this way many times before, he remembered, flying west from Toronto, where he'd broken in the first credit-card crews, to Vancouver, where the Red Circle was a top player in spite of the authorities.

Now, seated comfortably on Air Canada Flight 688, Gee Sin was cruising at twenty thousand feet, descending toward Vancouver, for a two-night layover before the long flight back to Hong Kong. He saw the Canadian coastline below and took a deep breath, as if a weight had been removed. He was already out, out of the United States, out of American airspace, out of its legal jurisdiction. Out of sight and out of mind.

He would not be present for any investigation into the shootings over the bus routes, or the bad blood between the Fukienese crews, or the feuding tongs. The Red Circle's financial involvement would be on hold until the Fukienese side cleaned up its own house.

The attention that the shootings brought was disappointing. *Best to postpone for now.*

Credit-card operations in the numerous cities would proceed as scheduled.

While descending, Sin considered the Chinatown murder

of Uncle Four, and decided that the matter of the stolen gold pandas and diamonds would be given to Grass Sandal. He would be instructed to arrange a meeting with the Chinatown limousine driver whom the New York City police had in custody. The incarcerated driver could provide details and clues leading to the missing mistress.

Best to do it from Hong Kong, he thought, where he had vastly more control of matters.

One of the triad's law firms could start the necessary legal machinery needed to obtain the interview from there.

Otherwise, the holiday had been going well. A handful of *shoppers* had been arrested, as expected, but the majority were bringing in significant sums. Besides, shoppers could be recruited everywhere; they were expendable.

The volume from the phone and mail-order houses surpassed even his expectations. Grass Sandal had had to close or vacate several receiving locations because they'd filled up with electronic swag after they had been used for a number of weeks. Millions of dollars worth of laptops, camcorders, game systems, cameras, computer software were consolidated for reshipment, then passed through the fences, stores they had arrangements with. The goods were converted to cash and became counterfeit Gucci and Prada bags in Hong Kong, hills of *bak fun*, white powder in Cambodia, then changed to currency again in Europe, Canada, America.

Cheat the people all around.

The strategy of the triad was paying off.

Courage

Inside the small Pell Street walk-up, Sai Go sat slumped on his sofa, considering Chat Choy's suggestion that they embark on another gambling junket. Sai Go wasn't hungry, and didn't feel like visiting Choy at Tang's Dynasty like he usually did, collecting bets from the waiters while he was there.

The battery in the bathroom scale had died, but he knew he was still losing weight. The cancer was feeding on him from the inside.

He powered on the TV, muting the sound to the Chinese cable program. The casino at Foxwoods was promoting a cabaret show with Taiwanese talent, Longshot Lee had announced, "sexy" singers and dancers in skimpy neo-mod outfits. The *hom sup lo,* horny bastard, coming out in him. Twenty-five dollars would cover the round-trip bus, a buffet meal at Woks to Go, and twenty dollars worth of betting coupons and store discounts. Gum Sook had countered with The Plaza in Atlantic City, also staging a Chinese floor show, featuring a troupe of beautiful Malaysian acrobats in holiday costumes. And the buffet was Chinese, not *gwailo.*

They'd decided on Foxwoods.

What the hell, Sai Go thought, *why not go along with them?* It's only three hours up the highway. It was a *gwailo* holiday but he'd just as soon play a few hands of Chinese *pai gow,* poker, or some *mini-thirteen.*

Many of the casinos offered a separate space for Chinese and Asian games of chance, featuring *sik bo, pai gow,* poker, or dominoes, and *bak ka lo,* baccarat. They kept blackjack and roulette action conveniently to one side just to keep the girl-friends of the players happy.

He imagined it in his head. *Drinks all around, brought out on trays by girls in gaily colored cheongsams.* Asian high rollers having a hoot. Winning sometimes and playing it up, but losing, mostly.

It was the last image he saw before passing out.

Afterlife

It was the bleating of the phone somewhere that awoke him. He wasn't sure if it was one of his cell phones, or the apartment phone. He'd left the lamp and the TV on; some Taiwanese soap opera with subtitles was playing silently.

Sai Go considered answering the phone but fatigue kept his limbs from responding. Then the answering machine came on. *House phone,* he heard his own hoarse tired voice on the recording.

The caller was Gum Sook, asking if Sai Go had decided to go on the trip to Foxwoods, that he could brew up some tea. "Call Longshot," he said, "if you want to go."

Following that, his cell phone rang, and though he turned, reaching, his legs wouldn't respond. He grabbed for the edge of the bed with his hands and rolled his body over. The cell phone kept ringing.

He was suddenly jolted by deep knifing pain in his legs, in his bones, knees, and ankles. He gritted his teeth, heaving breaths through his clenched jaw, until he could bear the pain no more and crashed into the blackness.

Into the Light

His view slowly settled on the clock radio as he regained conciousness. It was afternoon, a Monday, still December. Sai Go recalled the pain in his legs and gingerly moved them. Surprisingly, they carried him off the sofa as if nothing had happened. Relieved, he went to the bathroom sink, splashed water on his face. *Painkillers,* he was thinking, *in case it comes back. They'd surely have something at the clinic.*

He thought of returning Gum Sook's call. He resolved to *jup sau may,* tie up loose ends. He'd withdraw his twenty-five thousand and close his account at U.S. Asia. He'd like to collect his last debts at OTB, from Lum Kee the fish-ball vendor, and two waiters at Garden Palace.

Send a card to the *chun chik,* relatives, in Honk Kong. Spread the word. He, *Fong Sai Yook,* has passed.

Maybe place an ad in the Chinese obituaries.

Return the packs of telephone calling cards to Big Chuck Chan.

Visit Lo Fay, the all-purpose lawyer at the association's Credit Union. He was good for immigration, divorces, and other loose ends.

He'd ask Gum Sook to call and look in on him twice a week, to report the death when the time came. He'd arrange a cash incentive for Gum Sook.

Sai Go gargled, coughed, and spat into the sink, rinsing from the faucet without looking for blood in the spittle.

He put on his cheap down jacket and went down the stairs, exiting onto the street in the direction of the health clinic, and OTB.

The Price of Freedom

Inside the New Canton, KeeKee spread open the *China Post* and explained the racing results to Bo. She slid her French-tipped nail down the newsprint until she came to the eighth race.

"Here," she said, *"American Freedom.* Paid one hundred eighty-eight to show."

"My horse won?" Bo exclaimed.

"No, but *you* won anyway. For coming in second."

"I won by coming in second?" Bo asked, incredulous.

KeeKee laughed. "Don't worry about it. I'll cash it for you when I go for lunch."

Bo thought of Sai Go, wanting to thank him, to share the lucky winnings. She considered treating him to *yum cha, dim sum,* or a box of Fei Dong pastries, when he showed up for his next haircut.

Dead Man Walking

Doyers Street was an icy slope and Sai Go stepped carefully over the slick compressed snow. He followed the twisting street until he came to the narrow alley that split out behind the

Bowery, the same alley used by Hip Ching hatchetmen in their bloody forays against tong rivals, sixty years before. Nowadays, the alley was commonly used as a shortcut from Doyers to Chatham Square, leading out to the Bowery.

Less snow had accumulated in the alley. Sai Go exited from the gap between buildings next to OTB, a half block from the health clinic.

OTB looked crowded and he decided to stop by on the way back from the clinic.

The health clinic was closing, and Sai Go could only explain his painful episode to the technician, who apologized that he was not authorized to dispense medications. The clinic doctor would return the following afternoon.

Walking back, he saw that the vestibule of OTB had emptied.

Inside, he found the two waiters and collected from them, waiting around afterward for the street vendors. He stood at the far end of the floor, scanning the crowd milling about for the next race. In the tubercular air, he resisted the urge to cough, afraid that his phlegm would show bloody red. His thoughts strayed dizzily to a commotion on the betting floor. A curse rang out and immediately became *madda focker* in six dialects. A group of market workers laughed, and a construction crew cheered.

He didn't see any street vendors and was heading toward the front of the parlor when Koo Jai, appearing frazzled, tramped through the doors.

Koo Jai immediately spotted Sai Go and came toward him angrily. Looking around, he hissed, "You fuckin' complain to the *dailo,* hah?" Noticing the eyes around them, stealing glances their way, Koo Jai leaned toward Sai Go and whispered, "You watch your fuckin' back, old man."

Sai Go stood silent a moment watching pretty-boy Koo stomp out of OTB.

He laughed quietly to himself. *Ha, threatening a dead man, the irony of it.* Still, he was insulted by the threat and resolved to get his gun out of the lock box and carry it in his coat pocket. He knew he was sure to die.

But he sure wasn't going to lose face.

Gain, No Pain

Sai Go put down the cup of *guk fa,* chrysanthemum tea, and opened the metal box, empty now except for his run money wad of hundreds, and the Vigilante revolver in its holster. He took the gun out of the holster, flipped the barrel out to confirm that six bullets were nesting there, then pressed the barrel back in with a click of his thumb.

He put the Vigilante into the right cargo pocket of his down jacket. He didn't bother to take extra bullets. Whatever was going to happen wasn't going beyond the six he had chambered.

When he finished the *guk fa* he decided it was late enough in the afternoon to check out the health clinic. He stretched his legs, remembering the agony he'd felt, and wished he had a god to pray to, for painkillers.

No god; the doctor would have to do.

It was all coming apart, he thought. *How much more time did he have before the pain and sorrow bled out? Or was it all a dark killing shadow, spreading out behind the bitterness and despair, that no amount of time or forgiveness could cure?*

Bookie man. He felt his essence shrinking, becoming like a *teng jai,* sampan, in a dark tossing ocean.

In the beginning, he had felt that it wasn't a crime. He was just making a living, taking bets. Allowing the Chinese *hindaai,* brothers, to chase their dreams. Chinese were superstitious and loved to gamble. Who was the victim in that? The families or the associations usually resolved any problems that arose.

Now, after a dozen years, crushed by this fatal sickness, he finally saw it for what it was.

An underground life full of careless sins, chasing the dragon of good fortune. The dragon was devouring him from inside now. All part of the same evil. He was part of the trail of dirty money that travels in a circle. Money from gambling that makes its way to the pockets of gangsters. Money that translates into *bak fun,* white powder, and guns. Money that finances the smugglers of human cargo, feeding into slavery, prostitution. Becoming money again in the banks, the vicious cycle turning without end.

Fresh Money

Lucky left Kongo and Lefty by the front door of Number Seventeen's basement to cover the mid-afternoon delivery of that evening's bank; a brown envelope containing the usual denominations of dead presidents and statesmen: Hamiltons, Jacksons, Grants, and Franklins. The On Yee house manager and the courier walked past Lucky and disappeared into a back office.

Maybe it was because the new year and the new stable of whores at Angelina's had put him in a generous mood, but Lucky had had a change of heart; he was going to play wayward Koo Jai another way.

Copping a plea on the phone, Koo had told him he'd raised nine thousand cash, but he'd admitted he had only the remaining watches to make up the balance, although he claimed their value would be greater than the twenty K the *dailo* demanded.

Lucky had already figured he would take the cash for himself; he would let Lefty fence the remaining watches through his cousin's shop in Toronto. Kongo would mule the watches north. They would split the proceeds.

He heard Lefty laugh as he and Kongo popped Ecstasy pills.

Lucky had answered Koo, "Okay, bring the *shit*. And bring the boyz, too. Let's have a sit-down." He wanted to keep them away from the heart of Chinatown to cut down the chances of the other crews noticing them.

"OTB," he said, "At four-thirty o'clock tomorrow. And don't fuckin' make me wait."

Legal End

Jack spent days following the arrests of the Hong boy's killers at Hogan Place with the assistant district attorneys, starting the numbing grind that was due process.

At week's end, Jack returned to Cabrini where they removed his stitches. There were two small scars on the left side of his chest, in the fleshy tissue slightly above but flanking the nipple. The little .22 bullet had passed through. Further down were the puncture scars on his left forearm, rounded indentations where the pit bull's sharp teeth had clamped on. *Fuckin' mad dog.*

Pasini called, reminding him of his appointment with the department shrink. Standard procedure after suffering serious wounds in the line of duty. *No, dying in some stinking hallway in the ghetto housing projects was not how he saw himself finishing out the job.* The arm was one thing, but the chest wound above the heart was a *warning*, somehow. Yet any doubts he nursed made him less a cop, and he wasn't looking for a disability deal.

Afterward, after trudging through the thickening snow, he'd met Alexandra at Tsunami, halfway between her Loisaida storefront and the NoHo precinct house. They drank sake and Sapporo, picked from the sushi and sashimi on the little wooden boats that passed by on the mini-conveyor belt that ran the length of the bar.

"It's in the hands of the prosecutors," Jack said, "The punks basically turned on each other and implicated one another."

Alex broke out cigarettes and they lit up together, their conversation bracketed by puffs.

"We got oral and written statements," Jack continued, after

touching glasses with Alex in a silent toast. "DNA matchups on all three," Alex smiled sadly. "The murder weapons. Prints all over." He was quiet a moment, his stare going long distance as he said, "The victim . . . he put up a helluva fight. Wasn't enough. But he left sufficient evidence to hang them all."

Alex put her hand over his, her eyes misting. She tapped her glass against his again, brought him back into the moment.

"What does your friend at Legal Aid think?" Jack asked.

"Defense," she exhaled. "They may contend the original entry and search was illegal. No cause."

He'd been following up a missing person . . . there had been the smell of marijuana at the door.

"Or they may request a change in venue. Say they can't get a fair trial in Manhattan, because there are too many Chinese, Asians, in the jury pool. They may want a Bronx jury, or one from Brooklyn. A judge of color, who's sensitive to minority defendants."

Technicalities and racial politics hacking into the case . . .

"They can delay, file appeals, assert medical claims, demand more evidence."

"This is going to take a while," Jack said, finishing his sake. "I get it."

They shared the last of the big Sapporo over *sunomono* and seaweed salad.

Outside, the wind gusted up and rattled the big picture windows.

Jack paid the tab and they tapped glasses at the last swallow, with Alex saying "Happy New Year. To 1995."

"Yeah, Happy New Year," Jack answered with a forced smile.

They drained their glasses.

They caught a cab, and he dropped her off at Confucius Towers before going on to Sunset Park. They had traded cheek kisses and awkward looks afterward, finally shaking hands before she tiptoed through the snow and faded into the lobby of the high-rise.

Crossing the Manhattan Bridge to Brooklyn, Jack remembered the dead delivery boy. It didn't feel like 1995 was going to be a happy new year.

Storm

The blizzard roared in overnight, an arctic juggernaut that blasted in from the northeast. Fifty mile gusts toppled tall trees onto rooftops and cars, ripping down power lines in the darkness. Half of Long Island and Staten Island were blacked out.

NYC Transit rolled out two thousand snow plows, hundreds of salt spreaders. Sanitation pressed its two thousand men into twelve-hour shifts against the blowing two-foot drifts.

The outer boroughs were flogged by the swirling whiteout.

The airports were snowbound, hundreds of flights cancelled, with thousands of travelers stranded at Kennedy, LaGuardia, and Newark.

Commuter transit from New Jersey and Conneticut came to a blinding halt.

The sub-zero overnight staggered to daylight, fifteen degrees. Wind-chill real feel was four degrees. The shrieking wind drove the thick flakes sideways. To augment Sanitation's efforts, the city hired neighborhood kids to shovel the main streets. Still, the blizzard locked down the city: schools and businesses closed, disabled and abandoned vehicles made highways, bridges, and tunnels impassable. Frozen signals and switches crippled the subways and metropolitan railroads.

In Manhattan, coastal flooding closed the Westside Highway and the FDR Drive.

A broken water main on Delancey flooded the avenue and side streets, forming a half-mile slick of ice that further choked southbound traffic. In the Chinatown morning, shopkeepers chopped at the ice and shoveled pathways down the slippery streets, forming walls of slush-capped snow along the curb. Every so often a gap, a cutout in the wall, allowed for passage to the other side of the street. Fire hydrants were cleared; the Chinese were pragmatic to a fault.

Lunchtime was a trudging push of bundled bodies, hats and scarves wrapped around Chinese heads with watering eyes. Cars, trucks, and buses crept along, their exhaust trailing clouds of steam into the frozen air. Chinatown was digging itself out while the surrounding neighborhoods surrendered.

Death Do Us Part

They all stood around the couch in the front room, four distraught faces.

"*Dailo* found one of the watches here," Koo Jai admitted grudgingly. "Long story. It was out, on the bed, and he snatched it."

"Wha' happen? How come?" was the best the dumbfounded Jung brothers could muster.

"It was your fault," muttered Shorty. "You were careless."

"How the fuck do I know he's at the door?" bitched Koo Jai. "Fuckin' *nobody called me.* I could've put the watch away. *You* messed up by bringing him. None of this would have happened."

"Bullshit," Shorty said evenly.

"Look, it don't matter," sneered Koo Jai. "He said he knew we were pulling jobs. Said he didn't care. All he wanted was his cut. Said to bring everything we boosted."

"Hah, everything gone. No way," mumbled the Jungs.

"*Dailo* says we all gotta go." Koo Jai was steadfast. "Meet down Bowery."

"Where?" in a chorus.

"OTB. There's a coffee shop next to the alley."

"Why there?" befuddled Old Jung asked.

"Who the fuck knows? He wants a sit-down."

"*Deew!!* Fucked!" moaned Young Jung.

"Just be prepared," Koo Jai warned. "Keep your chins up, and your fuckin' eyes open. Unless *dailo* asks you personally, I'll do all the talking. If anything goes bad, we meet in Boston." He nodded at the Jungs. "Call your cousins."

They exited the flat, the Jung brothers jittery, as if they were going to a funeral.

Led by Koo Jai, they kept to the streets crossing Chatham Square; it was easier to walk through the dirty slush trails left by bus traffic. They came to the Bowery end of the square where access to the sidewalk was blocked by waist-high frozen drifts.

Koo Jai and Shorty were first to crunch their way through to the sidewalk, the larger Jungs behind them clumsily lumbering along in their wake.

Gusts of wind blew powdered snow off the street lamps and traffic lights.

The *dailo*'s crew turned the corner of Mott onto Bowery, moving in a loose triangle with Lucky at the point. Lucky saw Koo Jai and Shorty a half-block away, thought of the nine large in cash in Koo's pocket, imagining how he was going to drop some of it on some fine ass and pussy at Angelina's. Peripherally, he noticed the Jung brothers plodding behind them through the snowbank. *Clumsy bitches,* he thought, continuing on toward OTB.

Old Jung slipped and fell to one knee, the sudden twist of his hip dislodging the pistol he carried in his waistband. The gun slid along the dirty ice but he was able to grab it and pull it back. A few steps ahead, Young Jung turned and cast an annoyed look at him.

Kongo saw Old Jung dropping to one knee. He grunted as Old Jung's hand came up holding a pistol; it looked as if he'd pulled it out of the snow. Whipping open his trenchcoat, the Ecstasy pushing him, he went for the sawed-off shotgun dangling at his hip.

Koo Jai and Shorty both saw the *dailo* and his crew marching toward them. With their heartbeats spiking, they watched as Lucky drifted to one side. Behind him, the big Malaysian's eyes were suddenly as large as *don tots,* egg tarts, as he drew the chopped shotgun.

Lefty saw Young Jung staring at Kongo, astonishment on his face, momentarily frozen. Each of them instinctively reached for his gun.

197

Lucky recoiled at the sound of the deafening blast from behind him, his gun hand automatically going inside his blazer. He glanced back to see Kongo loose another blast into the ringing air and Lefty aiming his Nine. When he swung his eyes back to Koo Jai, both he and Shorty were taking aim at him. One of the Jungs was rising up from the snow, emptying his pistol at them in a spraying arc.

Lucky drew a gun from his inside pocket as Lefty fired mechanically, methodically, ahead.

Kongo dropped the sawed-off, drew his pistol, and tried to aim at Koo Jai, but the *dailo*'s back blocked his shot. He saw the short guy, the little guy, jamming off little firecracker shots at them.

Lucky felt the impact like a punch in the head, his body staggering backward. Suddenly, hot metal was tearing into him, twisting through him. *Fuck!* he heard himself yell, as his thoughts ceased.

Painkiller

Sai Go had crossed Doyers, was halfway down the alley short-cut when he heard the barrage of fireworks up ahead, somewhere on the Bowery. *Probably some fools celebrating the Year of the Pig much too early.* Two thunderous booms had made him recoil, the shock waves, he was sure, from China-made M-80s.

He kept his eyes on the icy furrows as he took the shortcut again.

Suddenly he saw Koo Jai, gun in hand, dashing at him,

running through the alley like a madman, followed by a short kid who was equally bug-eyed.

Sai Go's breath caught in his throat as he flattened himself against the wall, his gun hand sliding down to his coat pocket. Koo Jai raced by just as Sai Go got his fingers around the Vigilante.

Sai Go watched the short kid pass him, and was drawing the gun from his pocket when he heard the first shot. He felt an explosion inside his chest, sucking the breath out of him.

Several more gunshots rang out.

Then there was only abrupt silence, and the whiteness of the snow in the alley, drifting gently all around him.

O-Nine

Having covered for others during the holidays, Jack had returned to the day shift, feeling the bustle of the tour's activity juicing him through the storm's chaos into the afternoon hours. Outside the stationhouse, Sanitation part-timers cleared away the snow so the police vehicles could park. Jack took a late lunch, chowing down on a sandwich and chowder from Kim's Produce. In the last hour of his shift, the phone rang. An urgent voice from Manhattan South put Jack on edge.

"We got a *hot shoot,* in Chinatown. Multiple vics, near the OTB. See the CO of the 0-Five."

OTB? The Fifth Precinct?

The 0-Five, Chinatown, was pulling him back, back into the gutter.

Off-Track-Bleeding

Jack badged a southbound M103 at St. Mark's, scanning the distant stretch of the Bowery, seeing in his mind where it turned into Chatham Square, before becoming Park Row. He got to the scene in less than ten minutes, the bus driver skipping the stops after Delancey, until Jack pointed at the green facade of OTB.

From the bus he could see EMS techs in the drifts, lifting someone dressed in a black leather blazer and steel-toe boots. *The way Tat dressed,* he thought. When he got closer he realized it *was* Tat, bleeding from a head wound. The tech was palm-pumping Tat's chest as they snap-slid his gurney into the ambulance. Slush sprayed up from the spinning wheels, leaving a trail behind the lights and sirens speeding south toward Downtown Emergency.

Jack surveyed the bloody scene as the uniforms kept back the crowd that had gathered. Two more patrol cars arrived, blocking off the crime scene from traffic.

There was an odd symmetry to how the bodies lay: two on one side of OTB, two on the other, about fifteen, maybe twenty, feet apart. He started taking pictures with the throwaway plastic camera he always carried, locking in fresh images while waiting for Crime Scene to arrive. The big Malaysian on his back, a pair of startled eyes, was bleeding out under the sheet. The punk with the gel haircut, spread akimbo on a hump of snow, next to a mailbox, was Lucky boy's wheelman, the one who drove the black car. Looked like he had a chest wound. A fatal one.

The scene made Jack angry and sad at the same time.

Though he tried to keep his feelings out of it, he couldn't help feeling sad for Tat—not Lucky anymore—and angry at the gangboy's hair-trigger disregard for life.

A dozen paces across from them there were two other bodies, face up at the curb. From their profiles, Jack noticed a familial resemblance between them. Both had multiple gunshot wounds, including head shots. The wind kept blowing aside the sheets that covered them so he placed dirty chunks of ice at the corners to keep them down.

He picked up a blood trail near the entrance of the alley shortcut to Doyers.

The first body in the alley was that of an old man, slumped down on the sidewalk against the side of a restaurant kitchen. His right shoulder leaned against the wall at an awkward angle, his head drooped to his chest. His left hand rested on the sidewalk in front of him, like he'd been trying to balance himself. His right hand was in his coat pocket, which was twisted behind him near the small of his back. Jack patted down the pocket and felt the outline of a gun.

There were no discernible wounds.

He snapped more pictures, wondering how the old man had tied into Lucky's scene.

The second victim was farther down the alley, past where it angled off toward Doyers Street. It struck Jack as odd. A younger man, late twenties. He'd fallen forward, crawled, and finally died. His down jacket was unzipped, with an inside pocket yanked out. His right pants pocket was torn, a couple of loose dollar bills flapping out. Nearby, some coins were scattered in the snow, leading in the direction of Doyers.

The setup made Jack think robbery was involved somehow.

201

Knowing Lucky and the gang world, he felt the shoot-out had to be part of a Ghost Legion power struggle, over money, or face. *But nobody plans an ambush in broad daylight on a busy street, during a blizzard. Something unexpected must have happened, provoked by fear, or anger. Someone got nervous, and the situation exploded.* They were all Ghosts. Or were they just Ghosts in name, gang unity giving way to greed and jealousy, the usual.

Doyers Street was empty, the icy slush offering no clues. He crossed over to May May's convenience store, bought a box of ziplock bags and a fat black permanent marker.

He was bagging the different guns when CSU arrived. They proceeded to work the scene for evidence such as blood samples, laying down markers near the ejected shell casings, snapping pictures with their big wide-lens cameras.

Jack stepped back as the Medical Examiner's team showed up and started pronouncing the bodies. When they zippered up the black body bags, placing them into the morgue's minivan, Jack remembered that the commanding officer of the Fifth Precinct was expecting him.

He pictured the old run-down stationhouse on Elizabeth, three blocks north, and headed in that direction.

O-Five

He hadn't seen the captain in more than a month, since his promotion to Detective Second Grade, during the award ceremony at One Police Plaza, well after the captain had quashed the IA investigation, and before his transfer out to the 0-Nine.

When Jack entered the big office Captain Marino's expression revealed that he was about to do something he didn't agree with. He extended his hand.

"Welcome back, Jack," he said as they shook. "I have to say, it's not sitting right with me, to have to bring you back this way. Hernandez and Donelly caught the case, and rightfully, it's theirs."

Jack half-shrugged, knowing the captain well enough to keep his mouth shut. He let the commanding officer continue.

"But the chief's been all over my ass. The case is so high profile we need some quick answers. The street cleared out when the shooting started, and Hernandez and Donelly can't find any witnesses. Look, you know the players. And we know you used to be friends with one of the vics. The *dailo*, Tat Louie." The captain thought he saw disdain narrowing Jack's eyes. He looked away. "There's so much heat on this it's melting the snow outside headquarters."

Jack nodded knowingly, and let him continue.

"Chief wants the press off *his* ass." He gave Jack a look that was more a request than a command.

Jack knew what *high profile* meant. Shootings and gang violence always brought out the TONG WAR headlines in the *Post* and the *News*. The Chinese media, acutely aware that bad news would scare off the tourist-trade, the lifeblood of the community, would criticize the police for allowing the gangbangers to run amok in the first place.

"Get me *something*, Jack," Marino said quietly.

Jack, almost feeling sorry for him, said, "Okay, Cap'n. I'll keep you posted."

Hernandez and Donelly gave him the cold shoulder on

the way out, but Jack crunched his way back through the snow, following the blood trail in his head, to OTB where the uniform squad watched over the evidence.

Pieces of Death

The guns stacked up as a small arsenal: pricey Smith & Wesson nine-millimeter automatics for Lucky's Ghosts, cheaper Spanish-made Taurus pistols for the others.

Lucky had carried the 5906, a ten-shot customized hybrid with an aluminum alloy frame and a cockless hammer. It was light to the draw and compact, easy to conceal. *Tat, with his cool expensive gun, which he hadn't had the chance to fire.*

The EMS techs at Downtown Medical had advised Jack that Tat had slipped into a coma and was on life support.

The Ghost with the spikey gel hair had packed a 910 featuring an ambidextrous hammer drop. According to the ME's report, gunshot residue was found on his *left* hand. The gun was also a ten-shot piece, that he could carry half-cocked, ready for action in his quick-draw Combat holster. Dependable, and deadly. He'd emptied the clip, died reaching for the second magazine.

The big Malaysian had an eight-shot 3913 with a thick rubber grip for his large hand. A soldier's gun. The solid pistol never cleared his back pocket. Instead, his big piece of bad news was the double-barreled sawed-off shotgun, a twelve-gauge featherweight Japanese Winchester. He'd chopped down the stock and barrel, cutting it short so he could carry it beneath his coat. A nasty piece of work, sure to take fighters down.

He'd gotten off both barrels.

The other vics in the face-off told the other part of the story. All had soldier guns. The one in the alley died with a Taurus 938 in his hand. He'd emptied the ten-shot clip of the .380 automatic, an inexpensive import. *Great bang for the buck.* The bangs hadn't saved him from getting shot in the back.

Of the two stocky vics who looked related, one also had a Taurus, a PT11 racking ten shots. *Cheap but reliable.* He'd fired eight shots, leaving two in the magazine.

The other one had brandished a Ruger Redhawk, a .357 Magnum that weighed two pounds, a heavy carry. It was a *thunderous* six-shot revolver, and it's report alone would freeze all the action.

He'd emptied the cannon.

The odd piece was found on the old man in the alley: an outdated Italian model, Trident Vigilante. A snub-nose .32-caliber revolver that chambered six Smith & Wesson cartridges. Super light, less than a pound. A belly gun with a light kick. Good for close combat. *But why? An old man dying of cancer?*

He'd carried it in his jacket pocket without a holster.

His final moment had brought his hand to the gun.

Where was the connection?

Personal Effects

Jack made out the reports for the six corpses lying in the morgue's chilled slabs.

Lucky's wheelman, the gel-haired Ghost, whose street name

was Lefty, had carried in his jacket a set of keys in a black key-case, a pair of knock-off Fendi sunglasses, and a small spray tube of breath freshener. There was a plastic baggie with a dozen little red pills, and a murky snapshot of an Asian girl giving head. He had forty-four dollars, *an unlucky Chinese number for him,* thought Jack. In his jeans they'd found a cell phone, and a driver's license with a DOB dated 1970, and the name Cham Yat Lee. The license had a bogus Mott Street address. Number 17A, Jack knew, was an On Yee gambling basement.

The large Malaysian was identified by his Indonesian NRIC National Registry card as Bat Boon Kong, twenty-six years old. In his coat he'd had a pack of bootleg Marlboros and a Zippo lighter featuring a grinning skull and crossbones. He carried a hundred eighty-six dollars, and a roll of quarters. *Was he looking to pack a hard-knuckled punch, or was it just coins for the parking meters?* There was a pair of fake Oakley sunglasses and a business card for Oriental Massage Bodywork. A set of keys attached to a jade-stone dragon. From his pants they'd taken a bloody cell phone, identical to the one found on Cham Yat. Kong had worn a heavy gold bar-link chain around his thick neck, dangling a fat jade lucky Buddha against his massive chest, but there was no *ho toy,* good fortune, at the end of his story.

The other two dead Ghosts outside OTB shared more than a passing resemblance; they shared the same surname, Jung, and birthdate, in 1971. They were twins, but not identical. *Close enough,* thought Jack.

According to their driver's licenses, one was named James, one Joseph.

Jimmy and Joey Jung. The Jung brothers. They'd both worn black stone *foo* dogs around their necks, and between them they had fifty-one dollars and change. They had lived in the same apartment in the Rutgers Housing Projects out past Pike, near the river.

Jack remembered hanging out there with Tat and Wing during their teenage summer nights that now seemed so long ago.

Each brother had a matching set of keys, and identical blackface ladies' Rado wristwatches in their pants pockets.

Macho guys with women's watches?

The two watches were stamped with sequential serial numbers.

Of the two bodies in the alley, Jack wrote up the bullet-riddled *vic* first. His driver's license gave his name, Koo Kit Leng, and address, 98 East Broadway. Easy enough to check out; Jack knew those streets well.

Koo was twenty-six years old.

In Koo's jacket Jack had found a set of keys on an OTB promo key ring, and a cracked pair of imitation Ferragamo sunglasses. There was a pack of Kools with a disposable Bic lighter rubber-banded to it, and a roll of breath mints. In his jacket's inside pocket were business cards from a Tong Yen dry-goods store in Boston's Chinatown, and from KK's Karaoke club on Allen Street, with the name Tina and a phone number scrawled across the back of the card.

He'd worn a silver chain with a shiny letter **K** charm attached.

Jack remembered the two single-dollar bills protruding from Koo's ripped pants pocket, and the trail of coins scattered in the snow of the alley.

He had no other money or valuables on him.

Robbery or double cross, figured Jack.

The last body in the alley was the big mystery.

The old man, Fong Sai Go, had carried a plastic wallet that contained some business cards: lawyer, social security, hair salon, and a gold-plated Chinese talisman card. There was also a Health Clinic notecard with his home address and a chemotherapy schedule that indicated he was a fifty-nine-year-old cancer patient. *Terminal.*

He'd carried keys and a cell phone in his left coat pocket, a multicolored ink pen in the right. There was a Foxwoods Casino promotional card, in Chinese, in his shirt pocket. He was wearing a jade-stone gourd-shaped charm around his neck, and had exactly eight hundred eighty-eight dollars in his right coat pocket.

A dying old man spending down his luck? wondered Jack.

In his mind, Fong Sai Go wasn't shaping up as a homicide, but because of the gun in his possession, Jack felt he needed to check out the old man's Pell Street address, and also to speak to the lawyer on the business card.

Projects

The elderly woman who lived in the Rutgers Projects apartment appeared senile, or had Alzheimer's, Jack couldn't tell which. She managed to explain that the Jung brothers were her grandsons, and the food stamp card was hers. They'd done the shopping for her.

She couldn't grasp the idea that her grandsons were dead. *When would they be home?* They were her caregivers.

Jack decided to get her some assistance through Alexandra's contacts at Chinatown social services.

Hovel

Inside Koo's place at 98 East Broadway, Jack walked through a run-down railroad apartment that someone had tossed. A couple of pieces of floorboard were out of place, and the stash spots were empty. Nothing in the apartment provided any real clues to how the body in the alley had come to that end. There were only a few pieces of old furniture and some cheap ornaments of a life on the edge.

The landlord hid behind a managing agency that admitted Koo was a longtime tenant.

They had no idea what business he was in, but the rent was paid regularly.

The managers were interviewing new tenants even as Jack left the agency.

Sampan

He found old Fong's tenement walk-up on Pell, badged the super, and spoke to him in Toishanese, their common tongue. The swarthy man liked that Jack could speak the dialect and let him right into the apartment.

The place looked straightened up, neat. Nothing in the refrigerator. No garbage anywhere, cleaned the way someone would when leaving on an extended vacation. *His vacation was to the next life?*

The only thing Jack noted was a torn scrap of thin wrinkly paper on a VCR shelf. There were different Chinese nicknames and numbers written on the delicate paper. On a hunch, Jack licked his thumb and touched it to the scrap. When it melted, he grinned knowingly.

It was the kind of soluble paper that old-time bookmakers used.

Jack called the lawyer's number on the card, but only got voice mail.

He headed back along Mott Street, meaning to stop by later at Downtown Medical to see if there'd been any change in Lucky's condition.

Dailo's Demise

They'd placed Tat's clothes and possessions in a big black plastic garbage bag and slipped it under his bed by the respirator.

In a Gucci billfold, Lucky had carried an eight-hundred-dollar stack of crisp fifties, and two fresh condoms. Ribbed

Trojans. Slotted into the inserts were two credit cards, and a driver's license with another bogus address. Jack knew that number 29A Mott, was another one of the On Yee gambling basements. He was surprised that Lucky had used his real name *Tat Louie* on the credit cards.

There were three red pills in a little ziplock bag and a set of keys on a Cartier keychain. He'd worn an Oyster Rolex, Armani shades, and a thick gold-braided chain with a round medallion stamped with the Chinese word *fook,* or luck.

Jack remembered the medallion from their neighborhood years when they had been like blood brothers.

Tat's luck had run out.

They'd also bagged his cell phone, identical to the ones found on the Malaysian, Kong, and on Cham. *Courtesy of an On Yee corporate account, no doubt,* thought Jack.

The last item seemed out of place; a ladies' blackface Rado wristwatch they'd taken from his blazer pocket. Its serial numbers picked up the sequence where the Jung brothers' Rado watches left off.

The shoot-out was over watches, and money, more than likely.

Jack looked at Tat's comatose body and considered what a waste his old friend's life had been. *Punks, playing at living large; every one with a tattoo, a gun, and some pocket money. But not one of them ever had a future. Their days were numbered the second they signed on to the fast life, the easy money.*

This is how it ends for you? Kept alive by a machine only because we hope you have testimony to give?

The gang had fallen out over money. Different factions, different agendas. But *that* was expected, happened all the time in gangland.

Got anything to add to that, Tat?

He didn't think Tat was going to be much help but persuaded himself to stay a while longer. In the quiet room he watched the slow rise and fall of Tat's chest, listening for the occasional ping of the machine that mechanically measured out the remaining breaths of Lucky Louie's life.

While he waited, Jack checked the serial numbers of the wristwatches with Rado loss prevention. He was informed they were from the Hong Kong Region territory, part of a batch that had been stolen out of Sheung Wan.

Jack wasn't surprised that they'd wound up in New York's Chinatown.

He wanted to call Hong Kong but realized it would be the middle of the graveyard shift there, with their intel shut down. Instead, he returned to Sunset Park for a bracing shower and a change of clothes. In the bathroom mirror, he saw the scars on his chest and forearm healing nicely. Only then did he remember that Ah Por had touched those spots during his last visit, *before* he'd gotten wounded, when he'd thought she'd been confused.

She'd already known.

He felt the urge to visit her again, as soon as the evidence cleared.

At 9 PM he called Hong Kong. Putting on his best Chinatown Cantonese for the Royal Hong Kong Police, he confirmed off the record that the heist, orchestrated by the Red Circle triad, had been a quarter-million-dollar payday for them.

The payback had found its way down to six dead people in Chinatown.

Dead Men Talking

When he got back to the 0-Five there was a big file envelope waiting with his name on it. The captain had signed for it and left it on the desk where Jack had been working the case.

The Medical Examiner's reports were inside, a thick sheath of papers and photographs; six sets of clinical observations and explanations, one set for each victim.

Except for the old man, the other five corpses all had gang tattoos. This didn't surprise Jack. He knew they were Ghost Legion, *gwai,* Lucky's crew. Tat, Cham, and big Kong all had the Chinese word *ghost* tattooed onto their left biceps. The gang tats were black ink, but in different script or block styles.

gwai

What interested Jack was the tats on the other players: the two Jung brothers, and Koo Kit. Each had a quarter-sized red star tattooed on his back, just below the right shoulder. *An eight-pointed star.* Old tattoos, Jack could tell, because of how the red tint had faded.

None of them had the word *ghost* tattooed anywhere.

But they were all Ghosts, had to have had criminal records. Jack knew their rap sheets would blow their shady covers.

Jack noted the ME's indications that Lucky and his crew all had alcohol and Ecstasy in their systems. Again, not unusual for them.

They'd indicated gun-shot residue on Cham's left hand. A *lefty*. The other shooters were all right handed.

Jack remembered what a miracle it had been that no civilians had gotten hurt. *Thank the blizzard for that.*

The comparative reports from the Medical Examiner's office and the Crime Scene Unit listed Cause of Death (COD), *what* or *who* caused the death, and offered a tentative scenario, how it had probably happened.

They'd matched the fingerprints on the shell casings to the shooters, making it clearer.

Ballistics and Foreign Sics

Except for Lefty—Cham—all the other gang vics had suffered multiple gunshot wounds. Lefty had expired due to a single kill-shot wound determined to have come from the .357 Magnum revolver of Joey Jung. The magnum slug had drilled a hole in Lefty's chest and exploded half his heart out through his back.

Kong, the big Malaysian, had taken eight hits from four different guns; two in the chest from Jimmy Jung's nine-millimeter, two more in the stomach from Koo Kit's .380. Joey Jung had shattered Kong's right hip with two .357 Magnum rounds, but it was a pair of high-velocity .22-caliber slugs that had put out the big man's lights.

Two twenty-twos through the right eye.

They'd extracted the killshots from inside Kong's skull, where the spinning metal pieces had torn up half his brain matter before fragmenting, flattening against bone.

Jack imagined the scene with wicked clarity, tracing the gun battle in his mind, seeing all the players with the star tattoos exchanging gunfire with Lucky's crew. It had to have happened so fast Tat never got to draw his gun. *Thirty seconds, less than a minute.*

Jack saw a chain of actions and reactions pulling the gangboys along helplessly, like puppets. *Who was the first shooter?* They hadn't found any eyewitnesses. *Wait for Tat to talk? If ever?*

The Jung brothers had both been seriously wounded by the heavy scattershot from Kong's shotgun, but it was Jimmy who'd borne the brunt of the blasts. A dozen pellets had ripped open his chest and pierced his heart.

Joey Jung had three gaping wounds from the shotgun, but the two nine-millimeter headshots from Lefty Cham were what killed him. Except in right profile, he no longer bore a resemblance to his brother.

Koo Kit had taken two nine-millimeter blasts to his left shoulder and leg, sureshot Lefty drilling him, probably, as he was angling toward the alley. He'd made it partway to Doyers when four .22 hi-vels ripped through his back and riddled his heart from behind.

Twenty-twos. They'd recovered two slugs intact, in perfect shape.

Jack remembered the body sprawled near the bend in the alley.

The ME had noted that all the .22-caliber bullets had penetrated at an upward angle, as if the shooter was on one knee, or shooting from the hip. Since they hadn't recovered any .22-caliber shell casings, Jack figured the gun had to be a revolver.

Somewhere in the puzzle was a missing .22- caliber piece, and a shooter in the wind who was responsible for two kill shot homicides and a coma victim.

The old man, Fong, didn't appear to be a homicide. If he was, they'd never be able to prove it. The ME had ruled COD as cardiac arrest. Instant death due to a massive heart attack. *He never knew what hit him. A quick death, better than a slow one.* Who was the perp? *God?*

Closing the envelope, Jack called One Police Plaza, and then Manhattan South.

Most Precious

Bo was disappointed that Sai Go hadn't shown up that week. She'd brought in a box of *don tot,* egg custard tarts, and planned to take him to Golden Unicorn for *yum cha,* tea. She'd guessed that he'd gone on another gambling junket with his friends.

When the two men in suits came through the door, she thought they were walk-ins, even though she'd hardly ever seen suits walking into the New Canton. *A Chinese man and a white man,* quietly glancing around the shop. Abruptly, the Chinese man asked for the owner, and KeeKee beckoned him over, a curious look on her face.

They spoke in low voices, and after a few moments, all looked at Bo.

Bo's first fear was that the men were immigration agents. Someone had betrayed her and they were here to send her back to China, or to extort money.

She was puzzled when the Chinese man explained that he was a lawyer, and that he was a friend of Sai Go. The Caucasian man, according to the lawyer, was an agent for an insurance company. They had some papers for her to sign, and items to turn over.

The Chinese lawyer, named Lo Fay, explained that Sai Go had suffered a sudden heart attack, and passed away.

Bo trembled as sadness came over her. The jade gourd and the Kwan Kung talisman had failed.

"You are the beneficiary of his life insurance policy, and according to his will . . ."

She started to weep, and KeeKee put an arm around her, comforting her.

"Fifty thousand dollars . . ."

She heard his words as if from a distance, in fragments, unable to comprehend the numbers. She remembered Sai Go's last visit, when he had gifted her with the betting ticket from OTB. *He'd had a smile on his face.*

She trembled uncontrollably through her tears, and could not help thinking of her family in China.

"He'd had no relatives to consider."

She felt ashamed that she was already thinking about paying off the snakeheads, but she found new hope in Sai Go's generosity. She might finally bring her daughter and mother to America.

"Evergreen Hills cemetery," Lo Fay was saying, "by the new Fong Association section."

KeeKee told Bo to go home and rest and grieve privately but she insisted on finishing out the day.

She vowed to herself to pay respects in the morning, at Sai Go's grave. She promised to sweep around his tombstone every spring's *ching ming,* memorial period, at every anniversary of his passing, for the rest of her life.

At the end of the day, an old Chinese man came to the salon and presented Bo with a package, saying it was from his friend Fong Sai Go. She thanked him and he left. Removing the brown mahjong-paper wrapping, usually used by old-timers to cover the playing surface, she saw a polished mahogany box with a mother-of-pearl Double-Happiness symbol inlaid across the top. Inside the box was the gold-plated talisman card she'd given to Sai Go long ago. Beneath the talisman was a large red *lai see,* lucky-money envelope.

The *lai see* was thick. She opened it and saw neatly banded stacks of hundred-dollar bills. *Lucky money from an honorable caring man who'd run out of time.* She quickly put everything back into the Chinese box and left the salon.

Outside, the evening was black, and frozen. She cried all the way home, her hot tears mercifully wiping away the hopelessness that had shrouded her heart.

Intelligence

Reaching out to the Gang Intelligence squad, Jack was able to access the computer records specific to Chinatown gangs.

The Ghost crew run by Lucky had had serious charges filed against them that were mostly dropped, dismissed, or pleaded-out. *Assault, robbery, promoting an illegal gambling enterprise, possession of controlled substances, and weapons violations. Suspected in numerous assaults and homicides.* The On Yee was rumored to have good white lawyers on their payroll. Knowing this, Jack scrolled on and clicked deeper. Under IDENTIFYING TATTOOS AND MARKS, he entered "red star."

The Stars popped up, a dozen thumbnail pictures of adolescent Chinese faces. The Stars were thought to be one of many small gangs, the off-shoot younger brothers of outcast Chinatown gangs that had vied for leftovers along the stretch of East Broadway before the Ghosts and the Fukienese came along.

The Stars, with less than twenty members, had mostly petty

criminal records: disorderly conduct, petty larceny, attempted assault, criminal mischief, nothing as hard-core as Lucky's Ghosts.

Maybe they just hadn't gotten caught with the serious stuff?

Sometime after 1989, their activities ceased. Long-standing warrants for their top leaders went for naught. *As if they'd disappeared.*

The Jung brothers, appearing younger, came up quickly as he scrolled. They were six years younger, according to the dates on the pictures. They had been charged with criminal mischief and menacing. The circumstances were not identified, and the accusations were later dropped when the complainants declined to press charges.

Other Star members had also been arrested for criminal mischief, and those charges had also been dropped.

Jack noticed that one member of the gang, Keung "Eddie" Ng, was listed at four-foot seven inches tall. A shorty. He'd had a juvie file as a teenager that revealed he had been arrested for criminal mischief, for spray-painting red graffiti stars all over the interior of a Chinatown warehouse. He'd tripped a silent alarm. They'd also charged him with a B&E, breaking and entering, even though they couldn't figure out how he'd gotten inside.

All the doors and windows were still locked when the cops arrived.

Under IDENTIFYING MARKS, the record also indicated he had a small tattoo of a monkey, like Curious George, on his left wrist.

Finally, the address given by little Keung—"Eddie"—was 98 East Broadway, the same as the current address for Koo Kit, the victim who'd been shot in the back. Jack deduced that

Little Eddie was good for whatever had happened in the alley. *The vicious little twenty-twos, shot upward by a shorty.*

Ngai jai dor gai, mused Jack, *short people are cunning.* The Chinese say that short people are more clever because their brains are closer to the ground, and they see reality more clearly.

Jack printed out the mug shots from Keung "Eddie" Ng's file.

Loot-See Lawyer

Lo Fay, the lawyer, sat behind an old metal desk in his small windowless office. He wore his hair in a comb-over and spoke through a crooked smile.

Listening to the man, Jack saw him for the shyster lawyer that he was.

"He was dying," Lo Fay said of Fong Sai Go, his client and friend. "He had no one else to leave it to, and he thought giving it to her was the right thing."

"He was an honorable man?" Jack suggested. "He wanted to do something good in his life?"

"Right." Lo Fay kept the squinty-eyed smile on his face. "She was kind to him."

Jack gave him a knowing look. "What did Mr. Fong do for a living?

"He used to be a waiter."

"Used to be?"

"He retired years ago."

"So, what?" Jack asked. "He was collecting social security, or something?"

"I'm not sure about that."

Jack leaned in, saying quietly, "What about the gun he had?"

"I don't know about any gun," said Lo Fay, losing the smile.

"Why do you think an old man like him would carry a gun?"

"No idea," smirked Lo Fay. "Maybe he had no faith in the police."

Jack grinned quietly, made a fist, and rubbed his knuckles. "What *exactly* did he retain you for?"

Lo Fay took a breath, saying matter-of-factly, "To do the will, and to handle the life insurance."

Jack waited for him to go on.

"He wanted me to arrange immigration matters for her. Applications, like that."

Jack said, "And you have a check to show that he compensated you for these services?"

"I'm not looking for trouble, *officer,*" said the lawyer looking away. "He paid me in cash."

"How very *Chinese.*"

"*Everyone* prefers cash," Lo Fay said. "It's the American way."

"And you work for the Association?"

"Don't misunderstand. I only handle the Association's accounts with the funeral parlors."

"Right, the *death* business," Jack said knowingly. "It's a complicated affair."

"Lots of legalities when you die," he answered.

"Like *who* gets *what?*" Jack added.

"Like *who* follows up, *who* takes care of the spirit," said Lo Fay.

The spirit? thought Jack.

"You have to consider Chinese tradition," the lawyer said. "The afterlife is just as important."

Jack thought of Pa's death, and the cemetery at Evergreen

Hills. He leaned away from the charlatan lawyer, saying directly, *"You* know what it's like in the afterlife?"

"Well, no. But people should be optimistic at death."

Optimistic?

Both men were quiet a long moment, the interview at an awkward end.

Jack shook his head contemptuously as he left Lo Fay's office. He remembered the Kung family's murder-suicides, the brutal killing of the delivery boy, Hong, the bodies around OTB, and couldn't find any optimism about death.

Touch on Evil

The two watches taken from the Jung brothers ran like they were synchronized, accurate to ten seconds of each other. Jack figured that one of the brothers had set both watches.

The Rado found on Lucky had stopped at 4:44 that afternoon. *The worst numbers a Chinese can get,* Jack thought. Lucky's time really *had* run out.

Jack decided to bring the watches along, just to see what the old wise woman would get from them.

The little copper-colored slug was a .22-caliber long rifle round, a high velocity bullet generally used in target-shooting competition. Jack closed his hand around it, shaking it in his fist. The small piece of metal bounced around. *It weighed next to nothing,* he thought. It was barely bigger than a grain of *nor may,* sticky rice, yet the minute projectile figured prominently in the deaths of two people, and had reduced Lucky to a comatose state.

Wise Woman

He found Ah Por at the Senior Citizens Center, on a bench near the kitchen volunteers who were still ladling out the last of the free congee.

He showed her the watches first. She held them up to the light, frowning at the rectangular black watch faces. *Black. Bad luck times three,* he imagined her thinking. She said, *"Gee sin"* quickly, and made a flapping motion with her free hand, fanning herself. *Gee sin,* a paper fan. *Another arcane clue,* mused Jack. *Paper fan?* He knew better than to question further, and took back the watches.

He removed the twenty-two bullet from the plastic ziplock bag and handed it to her.

Ah Por cradled the little slug in her palm, bouncing it gently like she was checking its weight. She closed her gnarled fingers around it, and squeezed. Closing her eyes, she jerked her head slightly, as if surprised.

"Ma lo," she said distinctly, and this time it was clear to Jack she meant *monkey. Bad monkey,* just as he'd suspected, and was now certain. Keung "Eddie" Ng was the missing shooter.

Jack thanked Ah Por, folded a five-dollar bill into her bony hand, and exited the center through the crowd of old gray heads.

Wanted Person of Interest

Back at the 0-Five, Jack reviewed the Gang Intel files, and put Eddie's photo, tattoos, and name on a wanted bulletin that would reach out electronically to a million eyes, searching into the wind after a clever monkey.

Mercy and Love

Bo waited on Mott Street until the Temple of Buddha opened its doors. Inside, a recorded chant came from behind the large wooden carving of the Goddess of Mercy. Bo burned some incense, kneeled before the goddess, and recited the prayers for Sai Go that she'd offered during the night.

On the way out she bowed to the statue of Kwan Kung, God of War, and went down Mott Street holding back her tears.

White Face

Jack watched as the men in blue windbreakers shuttered every known gambling establishment on Mott, Bayard, and Pell Streets, including the mahjong rooms, massage parlors, and karaoke clubs.

The OCCB, Organized Crime Control Bureau, supported by state troopers, ATF agents, and U.S. Customs and Immigration officers, raided the Association headquarters of the On Yee, the Hip Ching, and the Fuk Chow.

While prominent white lawyers protested on the Associations' behalf, the cops arrested every known Ghost on sight, and also hauled in the Dragons and Fuk Chings for good measure. The brazen gangboys were made to take the perp walk for the news reporters, ducking their heads to hide from the cameras, trying to avoid the humiliation of extreme loss of face.

The blue task force raided Chinatown apartments, basements, and warehouses for contraband goods: counterfeit designer handbags and computer software, watches, cassettes, and bootleg cigarettes. Department of Transportation marshals followed them and towed away all the gangsters' muscle cars.

The 0-Five, backed by the outside layers of law enforcement, was sending a signal to all the tongs and gangbangers on Fifth Precinct turf, a hard-fisted notice that the NYPD blue gang was not going to tolerate the wanton violence that had brought embarrassment and critical scrutiny to their stationhouse.

The cops didn't really give a shit if the gangsters killed each other, Jack knew, *it was only politics. When the wind died down, the stench would return.*

The pictures of seized contraband and the perp walks were published in the daily papers to show that the police had flexed their muscles, and were firmly in control of Chinatown.

One Police Plaza measured its comments, still wary of the fickle media.

Captain Marino called Jack and thanked him personally for his assistance, wishing him well on his return to the 0-Nine.

* * *

The *United National,* Chinatown's oldest newspaper, ap-plauded the many Associations for their cooperation with law enforcement, for contributing to a safer neighborhood. Vincent Chin's editorial pointed out the need for Chinese community-liaison officers, and more bilingual civilian employees in the local precincts.

The headlines in the *New York Post* announced NYPD MOVES TO END GANG VIOLENCE, CRACKS DOWN ON CHINATOWN TONGS.

The *Daily News* printed photos of the dead gangsters, labeling them "modern-day hatchetmen of the new tong wars."

The Metro section of *The Times* printed a picture of Keung "Eddie" Ng, wanted as a person of interest by detectives of the Fifth Precinct.

Jack knew they meant Detectives Hernandez and Donelly.

BAI SAN, Paying Respect

January eighteenth was Pa's birthday. Jack went to the cemetery alone, bringing the pair of potted hothouse Dusty Millers he'd bought at Fa Fa Florist. The cemetery grounds lay beneath a blanket of white, hard drifts that had piled up against the sides of the old mausoleums. The headstones were covered by white caps already melting in the morning sun, trickles of water running down toward the frozen earth.

From Pa's gray headstone, Jack scanned the hushed ghostly scene. At the other side of the cemetery, on a hilly knoll that was part of the new Chinese section, he noticed a woman

pulling items out of large shopping bags. She was a solitary figure in front of a new brown-colored headstone, setting down
bright red pots of poinsettias, the only movement in the silent
rolling expanse of white snow and evergreens.

Flames danced out of a big tin bucket as she fed the fire
handfuls of gold- and silver-colored-paper taels, fake ancient
Chinese money. A red cardboard car disappeared into the
smoke, following the million-dollar packets of death money.
Paper talismans of numerous Chinese gods were sacrificed, *bot
gwas* in different colors and shapes.

Even in the distance, under the slanting sunlight, Jack could
see she was crying as she spoke her prayers.

The sight made him feel even sadder.

He turned back to Pa's patch of ground, placing his potted
bushes gently into the snow on either side of Pa's headstone.
The dusty gray leaves with tiny white flowers accented the stone
nicely. Touching his fingers to the Chinese words carved into
the face of the stone, he searched his mind for good memories
but could only recall that Pa had been a hardworking man,
loyal to his friends.

He torched the incense and planted the thin sticks.

He bowed three times.

Wordlessly, he pulled the flask from his jacket and un-
capped it. He poured out a thin stream of *mao tai* liquor that
melted a line in the snow. Then he took a swig himself before
resuming the final good-bye he hadn't had the chance to say
in life.

"Sorry, Dad," he said quietly. "Hope you find some happiness
up there."

He emptied the flask and backed away from the headstone.

Bowing again, he took a pack of firecrackers from his pocket, holding it while the sadness in his heart brought the tears to his eyes. He fired up his lighter, and slowly brought the flame to the skinny silver fuse.

The staccato bursts of the firecrackers were hammered by the boom of cherry bombs and the clanging of ash-can charges as the New Year's crowds flooded into Chinatown.

The Year of the Pig had swept in on the icy wings of the hawk, and settled onto a left-over foot of snow and slush. Clouds of gray-blue smoke floated up from the fireworks as the masses tamped down the littered carpet of red particles that covered the winding snowy streets.

Jack smelled the stinging bite of sulfur and ash, tasted the gun powder in the cold air as lion dancers in colorful costumes leaped at the blazing explosions. They were inspired by the clash of gongs and cymbals, teasing the thundering war beat out of the big wooden drums, driving out the evil spirits that plagued Chinatowns everywhere.

The explosions blasted through the smoky air, spurring on the energetic lion dancers who were stomping through the snow to the pounding rhythm of the large drums. The plaintive gongs and raucous cymbals urged the crowds on, provoking another rain of fireworks.

The lion heads appeared to be breathing fire, bright white flashes of light beneath the brilliant gold, green, and red decorations that brightened the neighborhood. He saw images of golden pigs in all the shop windows.

Outside the Tofu King, Alexandra, wearing a quilted red

meen nop jacket, stood beside Jack, soaking in the joyous out-pouring as Mott Street filled with people and became impassable.

The kung-fu clubs performed all around them, twisting and thrusting the multicolored lion heads at the red envelopes offered by the shop owners.

Billy Bow, using a fat cigar for ignition, launched a mat of firecrackers into the street.

A long golden dragon, held high on poles, wound its serpentine way past them, followed by a pair of lunging silver unicorns.

Everywhere, a sea of bright red.

Twenty-foot strands of firecrackers, strung from fire escapes above, blazed to a thunderous end, inciting the crowds below to cheers and applause.

The New Year was a celebration of family bonds and a chance to embrace new beginnings. *Wrap up loose ends, settle debts, clean the house, sweep out the dust, buy some new clothes.*

The Pig was the twelfth sign, the last sign in the lunar cycle, the purest in heart and most generous of the animals. The Pig was loyal, chivalrous, and believed in miracles. The year was characterized by honesty, fortitude, and courage.

In Columbus Park, volunteers had shoveled back the snow, and the flower vendors pitched their colorful bouquets under the huge tent of the Lunar New Year flowers market.

The benevolent associations sponsored Chinese acrobats, and produced martial-arts demonstrations in their assembly halls. Because of the snow, there would be a shortened Lantern Parade accompanied by the Chinese School Marching Band.

The On Yee Association bankrolled a Cantonese Opera troupe's performance at the Sun Sang theater, trumpeting a community alive with celebrations of tradition, culture, and family.

The NYPD had fenced off the main streets with metal barriers, and blocked out strategic areas for police vehicles. Crowd-control duties provided overtime cash for the uniforms, most of whom stuffed cotton wads into their ears, crinkled their noses, and held their breaths in the acrid smoke.

This celebration, this new Pig Year was foreign to them.

Jack spotted Jeff Lee in a crowd across the way on Pell, tossing firecrackers at a pair of bowing lion heads. Knowing that it was the monkey, Eddie Ng, who'd ripped off Jeff's office on Pike, weighed on Jack's mind.

Seeing Jeff reminded Jack that slick short Eddie was still at large. Jack had sent out bulletins to the various law enforcement agencies and was hopeful the *ma lo* hadn't fled the country yet.

Jack tilted his face up to the blue sky and felt the warmth of the winter sun. Around him, the crowd roared again as more fireworks exploded, and Alexandra clutched his arm tightly against her body.

Sooner or later, he knew, Little Eddie's trail would turn up.

Until then, the January sun felt good, and Alex was a comfort to him, making the possibilities of the new year seem open to fortitude, courage, and good fortune. . . .